"I can't continue to take advantage of you like this. You need to call the agency and have them send you another nanny tomorrow."

Charles could see she was serious. Her words were heartfelt. Tears gathered in her eyes.

"Melissa, what are you talking about? You're a great nanny. You're doing a great job. The kids love you," he said with a smile. He wanted more than ever to take her in his arms. To comfort her. To reassure her. To kiss every inch of…but he couldn't do that!

"Well, I love them, too," Melissa said miserably.

"You only fell asleep last night because your nap was interrupted yesterday," he said. She was looking down, so he cupped her jaw with his hand and tilted her chin up, compelling her to look at him. He let his hand drop and stepped back to a safer distance. His attraction to her was making him want to say things, express feelings he couldn't possibly be feeling after just three days in her company. She'd think he was coming on to her.

Maybe he was.

Dear Reader,

This month we have a wonderful lineup of stories, guaranteed to warm you on these last chilly days of winter. First, Charlotte Douglas kicks things off with *Surprise Inheritance*, the third installment in Harlequin American Romance's MILLIONAIRE, MONTANA series, in which a sexy sheriff is reunited with the woman he's always loved when she returns to town to claim her inheritance.

Next, THE BABIES OF DOCTORS CIRCLE, Jacqueline Diamond's new miniseries centered around a maternity and well-baby clinic, premieres this month with *Diagnosis: Expecting Boss's Baby*. In this sparkling story, an unforgettable night of passion between a secretary and her handsome employer leads to an unexpected pregnancy.

Also available this month is *Sweeping the Bride Away* by Michele Dunaway. A bride-to-be is all set to wed "Mr. Boring" until she hires a rugged contractor who makes her pulse race and gives her second thoughts about her upcoming nuptials. Rounding things out is *Professor & the Pregnant Nanny* by Emily Dalton. This heartwarming story pairs a single dad in need of a nanny for his three adorable children with a woman who is alone, pregnant and in need of a job.

Enjoy this month's offerings as Harlequin American Romance continues to celebrate twenty years of publishing the best in contemporary category romance fiction. Be sure to come back next month for more stories guaranteed to touch your heart!

Melissa Jeglinski
Associate Senior Editor
Harlequin American Romance

PROFESSOR & THE PREGNANT NANNY

Emily Dalton

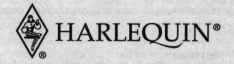

HARLEQUIN®

TORONTO • NEW YORK • LONDON
AMSTERDAM • PARIS • SYDNEY • HAMBURG
STOCKHOLM • ATHENS • TOKYO • MILAN • MADRID
PRAGUE • WARSAW • BUDAPEST • AUCKLAND

To my grandparents, Margaret Emily Rutherford Phillips
and James Jerome Phillips. I still miss you.
And you still inspire me.

Love, Sis.

ISBN 0-373-16964-7

PROFESSOR & THE PREGNANT NANNY

Copyright © 2003 by Danice Jo Allen.

This edition published by arrangement with Harlequin Books S.A.

® and TM are trademarks of the publisher. Trademarks indicated with
® are registered in the United States Patent and Trademark Office, the
Canadian Trade Marks Office and in other countries.

Visit us at www.eHarlequin.com

Printed in U.S.A.

ABOUT THE AUTHOR

Two years ago, Emily Dalton moved with her husband and two sons to Centerville, Utah, into the house of her childhood dreams. A two-story Cape Cod with dormer windows and a covered porch that spans the front of the house says *Leave It to Beaver* in a big way.

Her "boys," both in their early twenties, attend college within daily driving distance of the house, but keep busy with school, work and girls, leaving Emily and her husband plenty of time to spend together on their own.

Emily enjoys gardening and decorating, and she's still addicted to chocolate, Victorian art, Jane Austen and traveling by train.

Books by Emily Dalton

HARLEQUIN AMERICAN ROMANCE

586—MAKE ROOM FOR DADDY
650—HEAVEN CAN WAIT
666—ELISE & THE HOTSHOT LAWYER
685—WAKE ME WITH A KISS
706—MARLEY AND HER SCROOGE
738—DREAM BABY
783—INSTANT DADDY
823—A PRECIOUS INHERITANCE
926—A BABY FOR LORD RODERICK
964—PROFESSOR & THE PREGNANT NANNY

Don't miss any of our special offers. Write to us at the following address for information on our newest releases.

Harlequin Reader Service
U.S.: 3010 Walden Ave., P.O. Box 1325, Buffalo, NY 14269
Canadian: P.O. Box 609, Fort Erie, Ont. L2A 5X3

MISSY'S BEST CHOCOLATE CHIP COOKIE RECIPE

1/2 cup shortening and 1/2 cup butter, room
temperature
1 cup packed brown sugar
1/2 cup granulated sugar
1/2 tsp baking soda
1/2 tsp salt
2 eggs
2 tsp vanilla
2 1/2 cups all-purpose flour
1 1/2 cups semisweet chocolate chips
1 cup toasted pecans, chopped (See below for quick
directions for toasting.)

Preheat oven to 375°F. In a mixing bowl beat
shortening and butter on medium speed for 60
seconds. Add brown sugar, granulated sugar, baking
soda and salt. continue beating until all ingredients are
well mixed. Beat in eggs and vanilla. Beat in as much of
the flour as you can with the mixer. Stir in rest of flour
using wooden spoon. Stir in chocolate chips and
pecans. Drop dough by rounded teaspoons 2 inches
apart on nonstick cookie sheets. Bake 8 to 10 minutes.
Cool on wire rack. Makes about 5 dozen cookies.

(To quickly toast pecans, spread them on a paper or
other microwave-safe plate. Microwave on high, stirring
a few times, 4 to 41/2 minutes until fragrant and lightly
browned. Let cool completely before chopping.

This recipe will please the whole family, but leave out
the nuts if you're feeding a toddler! Serve with cold
milk and warm hugs.

Chapter One

"Dad, when will the new nanny get here?"

"Any minute now, Christopher," Charles assured his four-year-old son as the two of them stood in the curve of the bay window that looked out over the front yard and the street beyond. "And she's not really new, Christopher. She's just temporary, till Mrs. Butters gets back."

Christopher nodded, his carrot-red hair shining in the sun that streamed in from the bright July morning. He stood imitating his father, with his hands on his hips, both of them watching as an occasional car drove down Harvard Avenue at the sedate, residential speed of twenty-five miles an hour. But when a promising-looking minivan slowed down, then passed by without depositing their expected nanny, Christopher grew impatient.

"Did you say 'any minute,' Dad? 'Cause Sarah's hair's all tangled and stickin' out, and Daniel's got oatmeal down his pants and all over his face and hands."

"Any minute," Charles repeated, more to reassure himself than Christopher, since their fill-in nanny was already fifteen minutes late. But sticky oatmeal down Daniel's pants and on various parts of his body didn't seem to be keeping him from enjoying watching *The Lion King* with Sarah in the family room just down the hall, so there was probably no rush. In fact, Daniel would probably squawk if Charles interrupted one of his favorite scenes in the movie to haul him off for a bath. And as for Sarah's hair, he'd probably do more harm than good if he took a brush to those fine, tangled curls of hers.

Still…*where was the nanny?*

The temporary nanny service, Nanny on the Spot, had come highly recommended by his permanent nanny, Mrs. Butters, who had had to dash out of the house early that morning to catch a plane. Her father had died unexpectedly the day before, and Mrs. Butters was going to New Orleans to attend the funeral and be with family for a week. Charles had called the agency at seven o'clock, and was promised a nanny by nine.

If he didn't have a lecture to prepare for an important conference on Saturday, Charles would have simply taken the week off and handled his three small children on his own. Hadn't he done just that when Annette had died two years ago, leaving him with a month-old baby and two toddlers?

After the tragic accident that had instantly killed his wife, Charles had taken a three-month leave of absence from his position as Professor of Astronomy at Westminster College and devoted himself full-time to caring for his children and coping with his grief, and, with the support of friends and his sister, Lily, he'd somehow managed. But now he was back to teaching full-time—even agreeing to two classes this summer—and was up to his ears in research on a new invention. And then there was the lecture this Saturday....

Charles normally had a busy schedule, but he always made sure he had plenty of time to spend with the children. Recently, however, he'd probably taken on a few more projects than he should have. He was fully aware that having Mrs. Butters there to tend the children and take care of the household was what kept him afloat as a father.

Charles easily managed the basics of bathing, storytelling and roughhousing, but he didn't have a clue how to get Kool-Aid stains out of children's clothing, bake holiday-shaped sugar cookies with sprinkles, or comb Sarah's unruly brown hair into those neat little pigtails she wore. Nor did he have any idea what time the *Teletubbies* came on...though he *did* know it was Daniel's favorite television program.

What if the nanny didn't show up at all?

Christopher made an exasperated sound by blowing air through pursed lips and tugged on Charles's pants pocket till he looked down. Peering up at his father from under thick brown eyelashes that were just like his mother's, he announced, "I don't think she's ever going to come."

The expression on Christopher's small face probably reflected his own, which Charles was sure showed his impatience and worry. Determined to lighten up, he smiled and ruffled Christopher's hair. "What is that thing Mrs. Butters always says? A watched pot never boils? We're being a couple of watch-pots, Christopher. So, let's quit looking out the window and watching for the nanny and see if we can lure Daniel away from *The Lion King* and into the tub. I might even try my hand at doing Sarah's pigtails. What do you think, kiddo?''

Christopher followed his father's long legs out of the room, his own short legs hurrying to keep up. "Well, you can *try,* Dad. But first tell me...what's a watch-pot?''

MELISSA GLANCED at the car clock. It was already nine-fifteen and she was still several blocks from Harvard Avenue! She'd been promised the first call-in job that morning and had known she'd be working, so she should have set her alarm. She knew darn well it took her at least a half an hour longer these days to get ready in the morning.

Being eight-and-a-half months pregnant in July was no picnic. Her feet and ankles used to swell only in the afternoon and evenings, but now every morning she woke up with swollen feet, which made it rather difficult to wedge them into shoes. And if she wore her athletic shoes, which were the most comfortable for her back and legs, there were shoelaces to tie. No one had ever warned her about the difficulty of tying shoes over the protuberance of a nearly full-term pregnant belly!

Melissa sighed and pushed an already damp wisp of hair out of her eyes. The air conditioning in the car was on the fritz, and it was going to be another scorcher. But the heatwave and everything else would be much easier to bear if only there was someone around to tie her shoes for her, or rub that achy spot in the small of her back after a long day, or run down to the deli when she got that insatiable urge for salt-and-vinegar potato chips or a big, fat kosher pickle.

Melissa shook her head and smiled wryly at herself in the rearview mirror. There she went again, wishing she had a partner in this parent thing. But what good would a partner be if he'd never wanted you to be pregnant in the first place, cheated on you, maxed out your joint credit cards, and expected to be waited on as if you were his slave and he was King of Siam? In other words, if he was anything like her ex-husband and the father of her unborn child. No, she didn't mind getting her own pickles, thank you very much. Divorcing Brad was the best thing she'd ever done for herself and her baby.

Melissa decided that even thinking of Brad was probably bad for her and the baby, so she took deep, cleansing breaths and diverted her thoughts by looking out the window at an east-side neighborhood in the Salt Lake City foothills she'd always admired. Large sycamore and maple trees lined the curving streets, and classically styled houses ranging from imposing Tudors and Queen Annes to smaller, but just as charming, brick bungalows and English cottages stood at the bottom of deep, well-tended lawns.

Melissa wondered what kind of house this Professor Avery owned. All she knew about him was his occupation, last name, the number and ages of the children she'd been hired to take care of for the next five days and his address. She'd also been told that his wife had had to go out of state to a funeral, and he needed help while she was gone. Three children aged four and under, would definitely be a handful, especially for a working dad.

Suddenly she spied the address she was seeking on the side of a bricked-in mailbox. She looked at the house and felt several indefinable emotions at once.

It was a large Tudor with climbing ivy and blooming clematis covering a good portion of the front of the house, big trees shading the side yard, and the tops of other trees in the back swaying in the wind above the wood-shingled roof. While imposing, it still looked homey and absolutely perfect for a house full of children.

It was just the sort of house Melissa had always dreamed of sharing with Brad and the children they would have together.

Suddenly those indefinable feelings she'd had when she first saw the house became crystal-clear. Because of the happily-ever-after dreams she'd started spinning the minute Brad had given her his class ring when they were juniors in high school and officially going steady, the house seemed almost... well...*familiar,* and she felt envy and nostalgia and the bittersweet loss of those dreams.

Where had it all gone wrong? she wondered for the millionth time. Brad had been captain of the football team, and although not a sterling student, he was a star athlete with scholarship offers to several colleges, and the most popular guy in school. She'd been head cheerleader, Homecoming Queen her senior year, and an A student. They were the "golden couple" at East High. She'd been on cloud nine in those days, the envy of all her girlfriends, headed for a bright future. But the reality of her future had been a far cry from everything she'd hoped and dreamed for as a naive and starry-eyed teenager.

She'd been only eighteen when she and Brad had

married right out of high school. The wedding had been magical. The marriage had been a disaster.

To her surprise, Melissa felt the sting of sudden tears in her eyes. Angry at herself, she blinked several times and got rid of them.

Melissa drove up the long driveway of Professor and Mrs. Avery's house, turned off the ignition and sat in the car for a moment, gathering her composure as she smoothed out the seat belt wrinkles from the front of her maternity blouse. Why was she thinking about Brad and being so emotional and weepy? It had to be the pregnancy hormones, because she was *glad* Brad was out of her life.

Of course, it didn't help her general frame of mind that she felt so awkward and large. She envied the movie stars who were confident enough to actually flaunt their pregnant bodies on the covers of magazines...some of them not even wearing clothes! Maybe she didn't feel pretty because Brad had always chided her whenever she gained even as little as two or three pounds around the holidays. With an extra thirty pounds packed on around her middle— and, yes, a little bit on her fanny, too—he'd definitely think she was unattractive now.

Melissa snapped down the sunshade and looked in the mirror. At least from the neck up she looked the same as before her pregnancy. Today, though, she hadn't bothered to put on any makeup other than a dab of lipstick, and had had pulled her shoulder-length hair into a practical ponytail. Fortunately, although her hair was naturally a pale blond, her eyebrows and eyelashes were dark.

She snapped the sunshade back into place and opened the car door. Her backside stuck to the hot vinyl of the bucket seat of her compact car as she struggled to get out. Melissa heaved a relieved sigh as she finally straightened up, pressing her hand into the small of her already-aching back.

Then she remembered her nanny bag, a small suitcase well-stocked with fun and useful items to help her on the job, as well as a few jars of toddler meals from her fledgling business, Missy's Kid Cuisine. With a sigh, she bent over again, reached into the low-slung car and pulled out the suitcase.

Straightening up the second time was even harder than the first time. Clutching her suitcase, she shut the car door and headed for the house. She felt as though she was waddling, but couldn't be sure. She was teetering slightly from side to side...was that waddling?

Melissa scolded herself again for dwelling on Brad and put on a bright smile as she rang the doorbell. She didn't exactly feel bright, but she could fake it for the children's sake.

The door was opened by a tall, lean man in a green-and-white pinstriped cotton shirt, the long sleeves folded to above his elbows, and jeans that were wet at both knees. He had auburn hair and green eyes and was, in a word...*gorgeous.* His sinewy forearms were damp and sudsy and he was holding a chubby, redheaded cherub with rosy cheeks. The towel-wrapped toddler was obviously fresh from the tub and smelled like watermelon-scented bubble bath.

Melissa was beginning to think she really was asleep and dreaming, because this man fit so perfectly with her idea of a hunky husband doing domestic duties, and he was doing them in her dream house! Mrs. Avery was one lucky lady.

After a couple of minutes, Melissa realized that not only she, but Professor Avery, seemed at a loss for words. He was staring at her, probably in the same way she was staring at him. But he couldn't possibly be staring for the same reasons. She'd been struck by his good looks and obvious "good daddy" traits. Why he'd be speechless at the sight of a ready-to-burst pregnant lady in denim capri pants with a stretch panel, and a wrinkled white tent of a blouse, was beyond her comprehension.

Then it occurred to her that he might be a tad irritated that she was nearly half an hour late. "Professor Avery, I'm sorry. I know I was supposed to be here at nine," she said, offering an apologetic smile. "I won't be late again."

Still he said nothing.

She was about to break the awkward silence once again when he finally said something. Something she hadn't expected at all. "Missy? Missy Richardson?"

Melissa frowned. He knew her? And he knew her by her high-school nickname, the name no one but Brad, her parents and her two brothers still called her? But she didn't know *him*. Certainly if they'd ever crossed paths before, she'd remember.

"I'm sorry, have we met?"

He smiled. "I'm Charles Avery."

Melissa stared. He had a wonderful smile. Straight, white teeth. Sexy dimples. But she had no idea who he was.

His smile wavered a little. "We went to school together."

Melissa searched frantically through her memory,

but her continued silence told all. How embarrassing. *She didn't remember him!* But maybe she could fake it.

"Oh, yes. *Charles* Avery. So…have you seen anyone from the old gang lately? I confess I lost track years ago."

Now Professor Avery's smile changed from a spontaneous expression of pleasure to one of wry resignation. "If you're asking about 'the old gang,' you don't remember me, Melissa. We didn't exactly hang out with the same crowd of kids."

Melissa blushed. "I'm sorry. You're right. I don't remember you. Please tell me how we…er…knew each other."

"I was in your trig class, senior year."

Melissa remembered her trigonometry class. It had been a subject that threatened her grade point average. Her predominantly right-brained mentality had always made any sort of advanced math challenging, and she'd have never received a decent grade in that class if it hadn't been for—

Melissa's hand flew to her mouth. "You sat behind me. You were the boy with the—"

"Glasses so thick and round you could use them for hockey pucks," he finished for her, again with that slight, crooked smile.

Now Melissa remembered Charles Avery. But not like this… She couldn't help it. She gave him another once-over, from head to toe, from gleaming auburn hair to wide shoulders, trim hips and endlessly long legs in snug jeans and trendy athletic shoes. Could this be the skinny, shy guy with bright red hair and glasses that obscured what were obviously very beautiful eyes? He'd been shy and polite and incredibly smart back then. And very, very nice. In fact, if not for him...

"Now it's coming back to me," she murmured, her hand still hovering near her mouth. "You were the reason I got a decent grade in that class. You tutored me. You came to my house for three weeks, right?"

He nodded. "Four nights a week."

"Till I was finally able to comprehend what Mr. Daynes was trying to teach us." Her hand dropped to her side and she asked, not very hopefully, "Did I ever thank you properly?"

He shrugged, then shifted the cherubic toddler he was holding from one hip to the other. "Well, I remember something about some cookies—"

"Dad, is this the temp'rary nanny?"

Melissa looked down and noticed two little faces peering around Charles's legs. There was a red-headed boy and a little girl with a mass of curly, bed-rumpled hair so full of static it was sticking to her father's pants. She was still in her pajamas.

"I think so," Charles replied, casting Melissa an assessing look, his gaze lowering ever-so-briefly to her pregnant stomach. "They didn't give me a name. *Are* you the nanny we requested from the agency, Melissa?"

Melissa could feel her cheeks burning. She didn't think Charles sounded exactly sure whether or not he wanted her answer to be yes. As well, it suddenly occurred to her that Charles might be shocked to see her in this job. Back in high school she'd been president of the Future Business Leaders of America. Despite her slight math handicap, she'd always been good in business classes back then and had had big plans.

But look at her now! She was embarrassed. *Very* embarrassed. Charles wasn't making her feel that way, and she loved being a part-time nanny, but it didn't take an Einstein to figure out that Charles Avery, labeled a nerd in high school and excluded from her popular circle, had made something of himself, while *she* on the other hand...

At thirty-one she was already divorced, struggling to get the college degree she'd put off while helping Brad through school, and had to work a part-time job to make ends meet while she paid off debts from her failed marriage and tried to succeed at a business venture she should have started years ago. Actually, it was the things about her life Charles *didn't* know that were *most* embarrassing, so if she could keep them a secret, maybe she'd make it through the week without dying of shame.

"Yes, I'm your nanny," she finally answered, speaking directly to the little boy. "And I can't wait to get started."

Now she looked pointedly at Charles, who took the hint and stepped aside to allow her to enter the house.

"Well...that's great," Charles said, not very convincingly as he shut the door behind them and led Melissa into a large living room. He motioned to a chair. "I'll introduce you to the kids, then we can... you know...get started."

As Melissa settled in the chair Charles indicated, he and the children sat down on a sofa directly opposite her. Charles seemed to be trying to avoid staring at her pregnant belly as he introduced the children—Christopher, four, Sarah, three, and Daniel, two—but none of the children were shy about staring. As soon as his father stopped to draw breath, Christopher directed a question to the object of all their thoughts. "Are you going to have a baby or somethin'?"

Melissa smiled. "Oh, it's not a something. It's a baby, all right. I've seen pictures."

Christopher's eyes widened. "Wow. Already? But how—?"

"When are you due, Melissa?" Charles broke in, probably trying to curtail Christopher's questions as well as to discover for himself whether or not he had to worry about a pregnant woman going into labor while she was supposed to be taking care of his children.

"Not for two weeks," she told him, hoping he found that fact reassuring.

He nodded, but there was still a tiny fissure of worry between his eyebrows. "And...and how's Brad doing?"

Melissa should have been expecting the question, but it still took her by surprise. She had no idea what to say. Did she dare admit that she and Brad were divorced? That the golden couple from East High had had a tarnished marriage? That she was paying off credit card bills from Brad's extravagant support of his mistress, the rent on that woman's apartment and all the little trinkets he bought her?

Probably bored by now with the grown-up talk, Christopher scrambled off the couch, grabbed a ball from the corner of the room, and began tossing it in the air.

Charles returned to the subject. "He's probably

pretty excited about the baby…Brad, I mean. Is this the first for you two?''

That's when Melissa did it. She did it without thinking. She did it without considering repercussions or the very obvious moral arguments against it. She did it almost before Charles finished speaking.

She opened her mouth and out came the biggest lie of her life.

''Brad's dead,'' she stated abruptly. ''Killed several months ago in a car accident.''

Charles's face immediately reflected his horror at so insensitively mentioning her poor, dead husband. ''I'm sorry, Melissa. I didn't know.''

''Of course you didn't know. How could you?'' Melissa automatically answered, while internally rationalizing what she'd just done. *It's just a small concession to my pride,* she told herself. *After this week, I'll never see Charles Avery again. It's just a little white lie. A little…white…lie.*

Charles's horrified expression softened to one of sympathy and concern. ''I won't say I know just how you feel. People say that all the time, trying to be comforting. But, actually, it's possible that I *do* know a little of how you feel, Melissa. When Annette died—''

''Annette?'' Melissa quavered.

''My wife,'' Charles answered with a nod. He studied her face for a moment, then said, ''Oh, I see. You didn't know, either.''

''Your wife is—?''

''Yes. She's been gone since Daniel was just a month old. She was killed in a car accident, too.''

''But I thought… The agency told me your wife

was away to a funeral or something,'' Melissa explained faintly.

''They obviously got their facts mixed up,'' Charles said. ''But it sounded pretty hectic at the agency when I called this morning. It's my permanent nanny, Mrs. Butters, who's away at a funeral in New Orleans.''

Melissa was sick with shame! She'd told him Brad was dead to avoid revealing the embarrassing truth. She didn't want to admit that Melissa Richardson Baxter had made a shambles of her life. That she'd been duped and dumped on by her husband for more than a decade before finally seeing the light and getting a divorce. That she, the stupid, deluded half of East High's golden couple, had continued being stupid and deluded for twelve long years! But Charles's wife had *really* died!

''I'm sorry, Charles,'' Melissa said feelingly. ''*So* sorry.'' But he had no idea how sorry she really was, and for more than he could ever imagine. She'd claimed falsely to have endured a tragedy that Charles had actually lived through.

''It's been a while,'' Charles said with that slight, crooked smile of his again. ''I've got great memories, but I'm doing fine now. And so are the kids.''

Emboldened by the sight of his older brother having fun despite the presence of a stranger in the house, Daniel squirmed out of his father's arms and started skipping around the living room in his towel. Sarah couldn't resist, either, and got down to chase him.

Charles watched the playing children for a moment, then turned his gaze back to Melissa, his smile slipping away and his eyes darkening with renewed concern. "But how are *you* doing, Melissa. It can't have been very long since—"

Melissa shook her head vigorously. "Please, Charles, I don't want to talk about it. I'm sorry, but I just *can't.*"

"Nothing to be sorry about," he assured her. "I understand completely."

But Charles didn't understand, and Melissa was going to make sure he never did. It was going to be difficult, but for the next week she was just going to have to live with her horrible lie and hope Charles respected her wishes never to mention Brad again.

After a sober pause, Charles took a bracing and cheerful tone. "Why don't I fill you in on our routine around here as I give you a tour of the house, Melissa? We'll go to Daniel's room first so we can get some clothes on this little rascal." He grabbed Daniel as he scooted past, the toddler now naked as a jaybird because Christopher had stolen the towel and was swinging it over his head. Sarah giggled.

Melissa agreed to Charles's suggestion with a nod and tried to smile, but she couldn't meet his eyes.

Geez, I really blew that! thought Charles as he led the way to the boys' shared bedroom. *She's probably still too grief-stricken about Brad's death to talk about it. I'm not going to say another word about him unless she brings up the subject first.*

Not talking about Brad was actually fine with Charles. He was sorry the guy was dead, but he'd never liked him in high school, and the main reason was because of Melissa. If she only knew how he'd bragged in the locker room about all his sexual exploits with other girls, laughing indulgently at Melissa's old-fashioned notion about "saving herself for the wedding night." Brad had announced that it was fine if Melissa wanted to wait till marriage for sex, but he didn't share the same viewpoint. And if Melissa wasn't willing, there were plenty of other girls who were.

Yeah, Brad Baxter was Charles's idea of a first-class jerk back then. But Melissa had stayed married to him for all this time and now found it too upsetting to talk about his death, so the guy must have changed over the years. People *did* change. In fact, hadn't Charles's own physical appearance altered so much that Melissa didn't recognize or remember him when she'd first showed up?

But who was he kidding? Charles thought with a secret, self-deprecatory smile. Melissa might not have remembered him even if he'd looked exactly the same as in high school. After all, it had taken her no time at all to completely forget his existence the moment their tutoring sessions were over. She'd promised to come by the house with her special-recipe, chocolate chip cookies as a thank-you for his help, and Charles had waited for days afterward, sitting at home when he could have been out with friends, making sure his hair was combed, his teeth brushed, his clothes neat and clean.

But she'd never showed up.

And he never saw a single cookie.

He got over it, though. He realized he'd been a fool to allow himself a crush on the school's most pretty and popular girl, anyway.

Still…she really *should* have made him those cookies. It was funny how he still remembered that little slight, and how it still gave him a twinge of irritation and disappointment. After all, he'd given up outings with friends and his own study time to help her with her math. But as sweet as she could be—and he remembered she could be very sweet— Melissa was pretty self-absorbed back then. Or maybe he should say, *Brad*-absorbed.

Charles shook his head. High-school crushes... what a joke. In the big scheme of things, they usually didn't turn out to be very important.

While Charles dressed Daniel, he quickly explained to Melissa his busy schedule for the next week. He was relieved to notice, as they talked, that the children were warming to Melissa and she to them. Sarah, usually the most shy, had climbed up on Melissa's lap and was confiding something in her ear.

However, this didn't stop Christopher from butting in with his own questions.

"What do we call you? We call Mrs. Butters, Mrs. Butters. Are you a missus, too?"

Christopher had already jumped off the couch and had been playing and pretty much ignoring the adults when Melissa told Charles about Brad's accident.

Melissa darted a glance at Charles—it was the first time she'd looked directly at him since the dead-husband debacle—before she answered Christopher. "Yes, I'm a missus, too. But you can call me Melissa."

"Missus Melissa?" Christopher laughed. "Sounds funny."

"No, just Melissa," Melissa clarified with an amused smile.

Christopher nodded. "Okay. Are you a good cook? Mrs. Butters makes the *best* blueberry pancakes. How old are you? Mrs. Butters is *real* old. More than fifty, even. Do you have any other kids, Melissa?''

''That's enough questions for now, Christopher,'' Charles said. ''You're going to tire Melissa out before she's even here an hour.''

And Melissa did look tired. Oh, she was as pretty as ever, and while pregnancy became her, he knew the last month could be a trial. Annette's three pregnancies had made him well aware of that fact.

He just hoped she could handle the kids and all the work that went with them. If she stayed through Saturday, as arranged, she'd be within a week of her due date.

What was the agency thinking, anyway, sending out an eight-and-a-half months pregnant woman for a job like this? Charles wondered, frowning and worried.

And why did it have to be Missy Richardson?

Chapter Two

After the tour of the house—which was just as homey and commodious as she'd envisioned it—Melissa was again managing to look Charles directly in the eye for more than thirty seconds at a time. She was going to try to forget she'd told him "the big lie" and enjoy the next week with his three adorable children. His work schedule, as he'd outlined it for her earlier, would keep him shut up in his study for most of the day, anyway, or teaching classes at the college. She'd see very little of him.

While she wasn't dead yet—just pregnant and divorced and perpetually tired—Melissa was not immune to the charms of a handsome, well-educated, successful family man like Charles Avery. Under other circumstances, she'd like to get to know him better. But she didn't dare spend any more time with him than necessary, just in case the truth—that Brad wasn't dead yet, either, just dead to *her*—exploded out of her mouth in a moment of weakness.

While Melissa got acquainted with the children and the lay of the house that morning, Charles more or less hung around...probably to make sure it was safe to leave his children in her care. By noon, Melissa felt sure she had matters well in hand. She and the children were getting along great. Sarah's hair was in neat pigtails, tied on the ends with her favorite ribbons, Daniel was dressed and seated in his high chair squashing banana slices with the heel of his chubby little hand, and Christopher's questions were being answered as quickly as Melissa could manage.

As well, she was having no trouble finding everything in the kitchen necessary to make tuna-salad sandwiches for lunch. Mrs. Butters was evidently very organized and put things in places that made sense.

As Melissa scooped mayonnaise into a bowl, Sarah stood on a stool next to her and "helped" by sampling the pickle relish straight out of the jar with her fingers. Christopher still talked nonstop as he got the milk out of the refrigerator and promptly spilled some on the floor. Now Daniel was throwing his flattened banana slices—those that were still intact—against the wall, seeing which ones would stick.

Melissa was unperturbed. This was typical toddler behavior. Her back was to the door, but Melissa could feel Charles hovering and watching from the hall. She grabbed two paper towels, handed one to Christopher to clean up the small puddle of spilled milk, and dampened the other to use in wiping Sarah's sticky fingers. She finished this task just in time to catch a banana slice while it was airborne, then turned to confront her employer.

He seemed chagrined to be caught watching, but she just smiled and said, "Don't worry, Charles. I can manage. The kids will be fine. I'll be fine. But *you* won't be fine if you're not prepared for that lecture Saturday. Isn't that why you hired me? So you could get some work done?''

''Well…yes.''

''So go and do your work.''

He hesitated, then said, ''You're right. I'll go do my work. But first I should warn you, Daniel is a very picky eater. What he doesn't like he either hurls across the room or dumps down his pants.''

Melissa laughed. ''I see. So, does Mrs. Butters keep a list of his likes and dislikes?''

''No, because what he likes and doesn't like changes day by day. Each meal is an experiment, so to speak.'' Charles looked apologetic, waiting for her response.

Melissa merely shrugged. ''As I said, we'll manage.''

Charles nodded uncertainly, turned to go, then turned back.

''Oh, and they don't take naps, as a rule. Mrs. Butters thinks napping interferes with nighttime sleeping.''

Melissa smiled. ''In other words, she likes to maintain an early bedtime.''

''Yes, I guess so.'' Charles just stood there. He seemed to be stalling, trying to think of something else to talk about. Then he finally turned to go.

Melissa couldn't resist. ''Charles?''

He turned quickly back. ''Yes?''

''By any chance are you a picky eater? Do you have a list of likes and dislikes, and do you hurl food or stuff it down your pants?''

He chuckled. ''No to all three questions.''

She grinned. ''In that case, why don't I bring a sandwich to your study when I've got lunch ready?''

He grinned back. "That would be nice." After another pause, he turned abruptly and strode away, presumably to his study.

Melissa breathed a sigh of relief. She knew he was just being protective of the children—and of her, which was a wholly new experience for her, since Brad never worried about anyone but himself. But it was better that Charles kept his distance, for more reasons than one.

"What do you want to do after lunch?" she asked the children.

Sarah shrugged, licking a last, stray piece of pickle off her pinky finger. "We don't know."

"I know how to make play dough," Melissa offered.

The children's eyes widened.

"All dif'rent colors?" Sarah asked.

Melissa nodded, then motioned with her head in the direction of her nanny bag, sitting on the floor by the refrigerator. "Of course. I brought along some food coloring in my nanny bag. We can make the dough any color you want."

Christopher eyed the small canvas suitcase with interest.

"What else have you got in there?"

"Oh, lots of things. You'll find out, little by little as the week goes by. But there's something in there I want to get out right now." She retrieved the bag and set it on the counter, high above the children's eye level. She wanted the insides of her nanny bag to retain a certain mystery for them. She reached in and took out two jars of toddler food.

"What's that?" Sarah asked.

"It's food for Daniel," Melissa answered. "I made it myself."

"He probably won't eat it," Christopher warned her.

"We'll see."

Christopher's brows furrowed, his concerned expression reminding Melissa of Charles. "But will it hurt your feelings if he throws it on the wall or stuffs it down his pants?"

Melissa shook her head. "Not at all. Daniel can be my guinea pig. I'll try different foods on him every day, and if he likes something more than once, I'll know it's *really* good."

Sarah laughed. "M'lissa called Daniel a *pig*."

"No she didn't," Christopher scoffed. "She called him a *guinea* pig. It's not the same as a *pig* pig. It's like a lab rat or somethin'."

Melissa scrunched her nose. "I'm not sure that's much better."

Christopher stood on tiptoe and tried to see inside the bag.

"Do you have your toothbrush and pajamas in there, too?"

"Oh, no," Melissa quickly answered. "I'm not an overnight nanny like Mrs. Butters. I go home after dinner."

"Too bad," Christopher said with a doleful shake of his head, a gesture that looked too grownup and theatrical on a four-year-old. But, in just the short time she'd spent with Christopher, Melissa had decided he was intelligent and perceptive and curious beyond his years. Probably like his father had been as a child.

"I'll bet Dad would like it if you stayed and kept

him company after we go to bed,'' Christopher suggested.

Melissa was surprised by the alarming mental image that instantly sprang to mind, an image brought on by the innocent words of a child. She could see it all too clearly…her and Charles sitting by the fire, eating, drinking, talking, laughing, whispering, cuddling, *kissing*.

Yep, it was a darn good thing she wasn't spending the night under Charles's roof. She barely knew him, really, and she was already fantasizing about him. And knowing he was sleeping right down the hall would only make the fantasies more vivid and more disruptive to her peace of mind.

Melissa supposed that most people considered fantasizing a harmless pastime. But she was opposed to fantasizing, to daydreaming. After all, living in a dream world was what got her married to the wrong man in the first place, and then kept her married to him for far too long.

Yes, fantasizing could be dangerous.

CHARLES WAS HAVING a hard time keeping his mind on his work. He found himself recalling those three weeks thirteen years ago, when he'd tutored Melissa. The way her long blond hair fell over her paper as she did her sums, the way she bit her bottom lip when she was concentrating, the smell of her perfume, the way her face lit up when she finally fathomed that advanced math.

He was daydreaming. He was recalling old fantasies he thought he'd forgotten more than a decade ago.

Sitting at his desk, with the door to his study

firmly shut, he was getting absolutely nothing done. But at least he was keeping the promise he'd made to himself to remain in the study till six o'clock, the hour Melissa intended to have dinner ready…unless the house was burning down or some other disaster occurred!

Charles shook his head and smiled wryly. What kind of a schmuck still remembered a high-school crush with such vividness? After high school he'd gone to Stanford on a scholarship. He'd gotten rid of his glasses, gained weight on dorm food that he turned into muscle when he joined a gym, took up tennis and marathon running, and, finally, gradually got over his adolescent shyness.

In other words, Charles had enjoyed a full social life at Stanford and had dated numerous women before meeting and marrying Annette. He'd loved her more than he thought possible and was devastated when she was killed in that accident. Yet, even after many relationships and one wonderful marriage, why did he still remember his crush on Melissa with such clarity, the feelings he'd had back then so easily recalled and relived when she unexpectedly showed up on his doorstep?

Well, for whatever reason, it was inappropriate and silly. The woman was still grieving her dead husband! He turned his attention back to the computer screen and forced himself to concentrate. Five minutes later he looked at the clock. It was only two-thirty.

He kept wondering how Melissa was doing with the kids. He hadn't heard any alarming sounds to indicate that either she or the children were in distress. And he didn't doubt that Melissa was capable of performing her nanny duties. In high school she'd been the model of efficiency and enthusiasm in everything she undertook.

It's just that she looked so tired.... And he suspected she'd get the job done, and done well, even if it totally exhausted her. This suspicion of Melissa's dedication at the risk of her own health made it very difficult for Charles to know she was out there taking care of his kids, fixing meals and doing chores that on some days tired out even Mrs. Butters, who was the most robust, energetic, unpregnant fifty-five-year-old he'd ever met.

But he'd hired Melissa to do exactly what she was doing.

And she obviously was very sure it wasn't beyond her capabilities.

In fact, she would probably be extremely offended if he suggested she perhaps wasn't up to the job.

And she probably needed the money.

Hell!

Charles glared at his computer screen. Science had always fascinated him, seduced him, kept him occupied for blissful hours. Why was it failing him now?

BY THE TIME Melissa sent Christopher to fetch his father for dinner at five minutes to six, she was exhausted. They'd had a full day, she and the children. And she needn't have worried about any awkwardness with Charles, because true to his word he'd stayed in his study all day. She'd only seen him once, when she'd taken him a sandwich at lunchtime.

Now he entered the kitchen on the heels of his son, carrying the empty sandwich plate, glass and soda can. She sat up straighter in her chair and smiled, trying not to look as tired as she felt.

"Get lots of work done?" she asked brightly.

Charles first rested his eyes on her, then the table, which was neatly set and covered with dishes of food, and then the gleaming countertops, which she'd already cleared of the dirty pots and utensils she'd used in preparing dinner.

"Not as much as you got done, evidently," he murmured.

Melissa waved her hand dismissively. "Hey, it's my job."

Charles said nothing and moved to the sink to wash his hands. While his back was turned, Melissa allowed the perky smile to slip away. She didn't remember getting this tired even as recently as last week, when she'd had her last nanny assignment. She could have really used a nap that afternoon.

Charles sat down at the end of the table and smiled around at his three small children. "Whose turn to say the prayer?"

All three kids raised their hands.

"Me!" Sarah shouted.

"No, it's my turn," Christopher argued.

Daniel garbled something around the cracker Melissa had given him to nibble on.

Charles settled it, saying, "I seem to remember it being Sarah's turn. Christopher, you said the blessing at breakfast."

"But Daniel was screaming and throwing oatmeal the whole time," he objected. As if on cue, Daniel threw his cracker and let out a yelp.

"I think God heard you anyway," Charles observed with a chuckle. "If God only heard us when

Daniel wasn't screaming or throwing food, He wouldn't hear half our prayers.''

Christopher giggled, and the argument was over. Daniel, pleased with himself for making them laugh, grinned and remained quiet while Sarah recited the simple, memorized prayer that Melissa remembered saying when she was a child.

Along with Charles, Melissa helped the children spoon out their portions, but put only a dab of food on her own plate. She was too tired to eat. She pushed the food around, sampled a bite or two, and hoped no one noticed how little she ate. But Charles was eyeing her from his end of the table, his brow furrowed. Apparently he'd noticed.

CHARLES WAS ALARMED at how tired and flushed Melissa looked when he'd entered the room, and now she wasn't eating enough to keep a bird alive! He couldn't admonish her to eat as if she was one of the children, but there was nothing stopping him from making her go home directly after the meal and cleaning up the kitchen himself.

Above the clamor and conversation of the children, who were excited to have access to Daddy again after he'd been shut away all day, an adult conversation would have been difficult, and Melissa looked too tired to keep up her end of it, anyway. So Charles ate and enjoyed the food Melissa had prepared while listening to the children's detailed description of all they'd done that day.

No wonder she was tired! They'd done a lot. They'd made play dough, then shaped it into animals, made a zoo fence out of popsicle sticks and glue, colored and sprinkled glitter on cards for Mrs.

Butters's eventual return, practiced writing their names on the little chalk board in Christopher's room, and gone swimming in the blow-up pool on the shaded patio.

Charles gazed at Melissa with wonder as he listened to this amazing chronology. On top of all that, she'd cooked and cleaned and done some laundry, too…he could hear the dryer going.

As soon as the children were done, Charles gave them permission to watch a video and put Christopher in charge of inserting the tape and turning on the television. He left the kitchen with his chest puffed out importantly, his little brother and sister in tow. Daniel was sucking his thumb, a sure sign he was already getting sleepy.

"The meal was delicious," Charles said, as soon as he and Melissa were alone in the kitchen. "Just thought I'd tell you, since you couldn't possibly know from your own sampling of the food."

Melissa blushed and looked disconcerted. "Oh no. You're wrong. I eat while I cook. I was full before I even sat down."

Charles propped his elbows on the table and leaned forward. "I don't believe you. Annette ate as much as I did while she was pregnant…sometimes more. She was always hungry. She said food just tasted better and it was obvious she enjoyed every bite. I loved watching her eat."

Melissa stared at Charles. Now it was her turn not to believe *him*. Brad would never have encouraged her to eat or have enjoyed watching her. He was too paranoid about her getting fat.

"I'm just not hungry tonight," she said finally.

"Why don't you just admit you're too tired to eat?" Charles suggested.

Melissa stared at her plate, anxiety welling up in her. He was right, but if she admitted he was right, would he think she was too pregnant for this job? She needed the money, but more than that, despite the physical work involved, she loved taking care of Charles's children.

"I'm not going to fire you, if that's what you're worried about," Charles continued. "Or maybe I should say, I won't fire you under one condition."

Melissa's gaze flew to his face. "What condition?"

"I want you to take a nap every afternoon."

Melissa was speechless for a moment, then asked the obvious question. "What about the children? You said they normally don't nap. What will they be doing while I'm sleeping?"

"I'll watch them for an hour every afternoon."

"But your—"

"I'll get my paper done. Don't worry. You kept them so busy today, they'll probably fall asleep before the sun goes down and I'll have all this evening to work on the paper."

Melissa shook her head. "You're being very considerate," she said quietly. She wasn't used to that.

"Annette was pregnant three times. I know how tired women can get at this stage of a pregnancy. I really don't mind helping out." He slapped his hands on the table and stood up. "Which is also why I'm going to do these dishes and you're going to go straight home."

Melissa sprang to her feet. Or at least she was in the process of springing to her feet, but found herself still sitting in the chair by the time Charles had risen and walked around to her end of the table. "I can't let you do that!" she objected, peering up at him and marveling that he appeared even taller from this vantage point, which was on a level with his belt buckle. "Come on, Charles! I'm perfectly capable of washing a few dishes!"

"Tomorrow you can wash dishes because you will have had your nap and have a little energy left by this time of the day. Tonight, Melissa, just go home."

Charles's hands rested lightly on his hips, drawing Melissa's gaze most reluctantly to the slim perfection of those hips. She also couldn't help but notice his stomach, flat as a pancake even after a meal. Brad had been a physical marvel in high school and maintained his fitness as long as he played football in college, but after he was dropped from the team at the University of Utah for not keeping up his grades, he quickly developed a gut. Too much armchair football and beer.

Melissa dropped her gaze to her hands, the fingers puffy and pink from dishwater and pregnancy-related water retention. She was indeed tired and there was no reason not to take Charles up on his offer. She was touched by his consideration, but also conflicted. She wanted to prove she could do the job, eight-and-a-half months pregnant or not!

She had a stubborn streak that was sometimes a good thing, and sometimes not such a good thing. It was probably stubborn pride, along with a hefty portion of denial, that had kept her in her marriage for so long. She just didn't like giving up.

''Charles, it will only take a few minutes for me to do these dishes, so—''

Melissa stood up, took a step, promptly tripped on something and fell into Charles's arms. It was the only physical contact Melissa had had with a man in several months…except for hugs from her dad and her two brothers. But this was different. *Very* different.

Charles grabbed her shoulders and gently returned her to her seat. ''Whoa! You're not fainting on me, are you?''

''Of course not,'' she said, embarrassed and angry at herself. Her heart was fluttering and racing like some lovesick teenager's!

''Then why—?'' His face was very close to hers and his gaze—searching her eyes and face for pinpoint pupils and a waxy complexion, she supposed—suddenly dropped to her feet. ''Oh! Your shoelaces are untied. You must have tripped on them.''

Melissa could have explained why she had been unaware of her untied shoelaces, but it was just too mortifying to admit that she couldn't see her feet unless she deliberately stuck them out in front of her. Simply looking down and seeing them where they usually were just wasn't an option anymore.

''Those darn things are always coming untied,'' she mumbled, wrapping her arms awkwardly around her stomach to tie her shoes.

''Let me do that,'' Charles offered, getting down on one knee. He smiled up at her as he quickly and easily accomplished what took her plenty of heavy breathing to do. ''Annette had trouble tying her shoes, too. And don't get me started on pantyhose.

It took her and me and a small crane to get her into those.''

Melissa laughed. ''Hey, I quit trying to get into pantyhose four months ago. It was when I went to—''

Melissa stopped herself just in time. She was about to reveal that she'd last worn pantyhose when she met her lawyer at the Grand America Hotel for a fancy lunch to celebrate the signing of her divorce papers. It had been a great day and a great meal, even though the pantyhose had started cutting into her waist by the time the white chocolate cheesecake showed up for dessert. She'd only managed two bites of the luscious stuff because the pantyhose just wouldn't budge.

Charles didn't ask her to complete what she'd been saying, but he sobered and quickly stood up. She realized then that he probably thought she'd been about to refer to Brad's funeral, that she'd last worn pantyhose at her dead husband's funeral! Oh, that damn lie was going to torture her all week long!

''I'll go home, Charles,'' she said meekly, leaving him to draw whatever conclusions he wanted to from her sudden capitulation. She was just too tired to care right now. And another slip of the tongue could be disastrous.

''Good,'' he said, then picked up her nanny bag. ''I'll walk you to your car.''

Melissa couldn't believe his kindness. She wanted to repay him somehow, and the first thing that came to mind was to bake for him. ''Charles, thank you for being so kind!'' she blurted out impetuously. ''To show my appreciation, I'll make you some cookies tomorrow. I have a wonderful chocolate-chip recipe that was handed down from my grandmother.''

Melissa was surprised when her spontaneously offered gesture of gratitude was received by Charles with a look of surprise, then a frown, then a fleeting expression of...*scorn?* ''That won't be necessary, Melissa.''

''But I want to. I really—''

''Have you got everything? Let's go.''

Melissa felt hurried as Charles escorted her to the front door and outside to her car. She snatched quick glances at him, puzzled by his closed expression. Since mentioning the cookies, his mood had definitely changed!

It was still sweltering outside and it was quite a shock to go from Charles's cool house into one hundred degrees of dry, suffocating Utah heat. Melissa could hardly bear the thought of driving home in her little hot car with only the windows and vents as cooling devices, as all the while she'd be trying to figure out what she'd said or done to make Charles suddenly so distant.

Melissa pried herself in behind the steering wheel as Charles waited and watched. He didn't look angry or scornful anymore, just rather stern. Maybe, like her, he was simply tired, she reasoned.

Melissa turned on the ignition, smiled tentatively and waved through the open window.

''Better get those windows up and the air conditioning on, or you're going to have a hot drive home,'' Charles advised, not bothering to wave back or smile.

Melissa rolled up the window. No point going into an explanation about the car's air conditioning being broken and her frugal decision not to fix it. He didn't look receptive to any conversation, much less something so mundane and pathetic, anyway. Once she turned the corner at the end of the street and was out of sight, she rolled down all four windows.

HOW IRONIC, Charles thought, as he watched Melissa's car turn the corner. *Cookies.*

He shook his head and chuckled, glad he was finally seeing the humor in the situation. It was history repeating itself.

He was smitten and couldn't help being nice to her, so much so that he neglected his own concerns.

She was promising cookies as a thank you.

Well, it would be interesting to see if she actually came through this time. But if she didn't, it wouldn't matter. Not like it had mattered thirteen years ago.

Chapter Three

Melissa lived in Sugarhouse, about ten miles south of Charles's place. It took her fifteen minutes to get home, but by the time she got to her building and climbed the stairs to her apartment, she was ready to die from the heat.

When she got inside, she turned up the air conditioning—which she always turned off completely while she was gone for more than a couple of hours—and plopped down on the couch directly in front of the window-mounted unit. She toed off her shoes and propped her feet on the coffee table. Sure enough, her ankles looked as though they were encircled by a couple of inflated inner tubes. When Charles had got down on his knees to tie her shoes, he'd been up close and personal with those poor, swollen ankles!

Melissa closed her eyes and rested her head against the back of the sofa, lamenting the fact that she couldn't have met Charles Avery under better circumstances. For example, when she'd had a figure, trim ankles and no ex-husband. Then she reminded herself that she *had* met him under those circumstances...thirteen years ago.

The baby kicked and Melissa rested her hands on her stomach, stroking it in a circular motion. She smiled dreamily. "Don't worry, sweetie," she murmured to her unborn child. "I don't really regret anything that got me to this place in my life. 'Cause I've got *you.*" Although she wouldn't mind if Charles was the baby's father and not Brad.

Melissa was shocked by this thought, coming unbidden to her mind just as she was about to doze off. After all, she barely knew Charles.

Melissa's almost-nap was interrupted by the unmistakable three knocks, a pause, and two more knocks on the front door that was her mother's calling card. Although she was tired, she was glad for the company. "Come in, Mom."

Pam Richardson swung open the door and breezed into the room, looking not at all hot or uncomfortable from the heat. "How many times have I told you to lock your door, Missy!" she scolded, then scooped down to kiss Melissa on the cheek.

"I just got home. I didn't have time to lock the door."

"How long does it take?"

"Did you bring me something?" Melissa eyed the Tupperware her mother was carrying. There were five containers and one of them looked like brownies. Suddenly she was hungry again.

"I brought you lasagna, tuna casserole, beef stew with carrots and onions, fruit salad and—"

"Brownies?"

Pam handed her daughter the brownie container and took the rest into the kitchen, placing all but the fruit salad in the freezer. "You ate a decent dinner at that professor's house, didn't you?" she asked over her shoulder as she rummaged in the fridge, then emerged with a diet cola. She turned, pulled the tab on her drink and leaned her hip against the counter as she took a long swallow.

Melissa marveled at how slim, vibrant and young-looking her mother was at fifty-one. She dyed her hair to hide the emerging streaks of gray, of course, but who didn't anymore?

Taking a bite of brownie, Melissa considered telling her mother she'd eaten a good dinner, but she never lied to her mother. She wasn't any good at lying and it never got her anywhere, anyway. Today's debacle was a perfect example.

She swallowed her bite of brownie and confessed, "I couldn't eat. I was too tired."

Pam immediately retrieved one of the Tupperware containers from the fridge, put it in the microwave and punched the appropriate buttons to heat up the food. "Guess you and the baby need some dinner, then. Chocolate may be food for the gods, but it doesn't contain all the nutrients necessary for pregnant women and their babies."

Melissa didn't bother to explain to her mother that she was planning to eat one of the meals she'd brought over as soon as she'd appeased her sweet tooth. But her mom liked fussing over her, and it made Melissa feel cherished. She definitely enjoyed that feeling these days, and it made her mother feel good, too.

Melissa's parents had wanted her to move in with them when she and Brad had split and she'd been faced with so many financial challenges, along with the pregnancy. But Melissa withstood their heartfelt entreaties to let them take care of her for a while.

She knew she needed to get on with her life as in-
dependently as possible. Besides, they still managed
to help her a bunch, especially with her business.
She'd have never been able to take care of the physical demands of carting her product to stores and
putting up displays without the help of her parents
and her older brothers, Kent and Craig.

"Thanks, Mom," Melissa said with a smile.

Pam's eyebrows lifted. "For lecturing you? That's
a first."

"No, Mom, for everything." Melissa was embarrassed when her eyes filled with tears again.

"Missy, what's the matter?" Her mom was instantly beside her on the sofa, her hand on her knee,
her worried gaze searching Melissa's face. "Don't
you feel well? Was this professor a tyrant who made
you work like a dog, then sent you away without
eating?"

Melissa gave a watery chuckle, dabbing at her
eyes with a tissue. "Oh, no. Charles Avery is anything but a tyrant. It's just pregnancy hormones. I've
been emotional all day."

Pam sat back and gazed intently at Melissa.
"Charles Avery? This professor you're working for
isn't by any chance the Charles Avery who helped
you pass your trig class, is he?"

Melissa was surprised. "You remember Charles
Avery?"

Pam shrugged. "Of course I do. I was very impressed by him. And he was doing a good deed for
my daughter—a mother never forgets something like
that. Besides, he had beautiful green eyes."

Melissa stared at her mother, her surprise increas-
ing with each sentence she uttered. "You noticed his

eyes were beautiful behind those thick lenses he wore? How come I didn't? Heck, I didn't even remember him after he told me who he was this morning...at least, not right away. I really felt stupid. But then he doesn't look the same, so—''

This time Pam lifted just one brow, her expression sly. ''So how does he look?''

Melissa felt the heat climbing her neck and, no doubt, staining her cheeks bright red.

Pam laughed. ''Missy, you're blushing! I gather he's gotten pretty cute. Too bad there's a *Mrs.* Charles Avery.''

Now Melissa felt the blood and the color draining out of her face as she recalled her horrible lie. Pam watched with alarm as her daughter went from red as a rose to white as a ghost. ''Missy, you'd better tell me what's going on. And don't fall back on the pregnancy hormones as an excuse.''

Melissa blew out a long breath and told her mother about the lie she'd told Charles. At the conclusion of her story, after recounting the highlights of the day from her arrival to her departure, she stressed, ''I would never have told him that Brad was dead if I'd known his own wife had died, Mom. It's just that I—''

''It was wrong to tell him Brad was dead, even if his wife was still alive...but you know that. But I do understand how it happened, Melissa. Brad hasn't exactly been good for your self-esteem, has he?''

Melissa's chin jutted out slightly. ''No, but I'm not going to blame him for the rest of my life for decisions I made of my own free will. I know I was mostly just naive and too in love to see things straight, but Brad and I are divorced now and he's living happily—I assume—in California.''

"I just wish he was farther away. Possibly Yemen?"

"That part of my life is over, thank goodness. I'm doing just fine, and feeling better about myself everyday. I'm just sorry I didn't have the strength of character to be honest with Charles from the beginning.''

Pam sat back against the sofa cushions, took the brownie container from Melissa and peered inside, mulling over which one to choose. "You can still be honest with him, you know.''

"What for? He might fire me, and I won't see him again after this week anyway.''

"If he's the nice guy you say he is, I doubt he'd fire you. He's lived long enough to know that people make mistakes. He'll understand. And what makes you think you won't see him again after the job's over? Don't you *want* to see him again? Heck if it was *me*...''

Melissa recognized her mother's matchmaking tone and immediately nipped that flowering idea in the bud. "Mom, even if I admitted to the truth and he forgave me, there's no chance Charles Avery would be interested in me.''

Pam gave Melissa a disapproving scowl. "I can't stand it when you talk like that. Brad really did do a number on you, didn't he? Don't you realize how beautiful and special you are, Melissa Richardson?''

"You're my mom. You're prejudiced. Besides, Charles could have anyone he wants, believe me. Why would he want *me?*''

"He wanted you in high school. Give him some time! The week has just begun and—"

Melissa gave an uncertain chuckle. "What do you mean, he wanted me in high school?"

"He had a crush on you, Missy. Didn't you know? It was patently obvious to me and your father, I can tell you. The way he looked at you, the way he blushed and stared and— Well, we just *knew*. He probably thought he'd died and gone to heaven when you took him those cookies to thank him for tutoring you."

Melissa felt her heart sink. "Oh...*now* I understand."

Pam finally chose a brownie and took a nibble. "Well, at least we're getting somewhere. What exactly do you understand, Missy?"

"Why he bristled when I offered to bake him cookies tomorrow. He was remembering that I'd promised him cookies for helping me with my math and—"

"And what?"

"And I never delivered," Melissa admitted with a sigh. "I'd forgotten about that, but it's all coming back to me now."

Pam frowned. "But I remember you baking cookies."

"Yes. And I had every intention of taking them to Charles. But Brad and some of his buddies showed up while I was baking and ate almost the whole batch. I meant to bake more, but somehow it slipped my mind. Maybe if I saw Charles at school, I'd have remembered, but he was never around."

"He might have been around, only you didn't notice him," Pam suggested. "You had tunnel vision in those days, Missy, and Brad was the 'light' at the end of the tunnel, blinding you to everyone and everything else.''

''Great metaphor, Mom,'' Melissa said drily. ''But so mortifying.''

''Bake him cookies tomorrow, like you told him you would,'' her mother said bracingly. ''Bake him a batch for being nice now, and bake him a batch for being nice thirteen years ago.''

''I don't know, Mom,'' Melissa said hesitantly. ''He might think I'm…you know…flirting with him or something.''

Pam laughed. ''What's wrong with that?''

''He might have a girlfriend.''

''He might not. If he had a girlfriend, he or one of the children would probably have mentioned her today.''

''Even so…were you listening when I told you I lied to him, Mom? That I told him Brad was *dead?*''

''And were you listening when I told you to tell him the truth?'' Pam countered, gesturing with the hand that held the brownie as she stressed her point. ''Do it, the sooner the better. And quit overanalyzing and worrying about everything and bake him those cookies! It will ease your conscience if nothing else.''

''Okay, Mom. I get it. I appreciate the advice, now pass the brownies, please.''

''Your dinner's warm,'' Pam objected, holding the brownie container out of reach. ''Stew before chocolate. That's the rule.''

''I promise I'll eat the stew,'' Melissa bargained playfully. ''But the baby wants another brownie and she wants it now! Can't you feel her kicking?'' She took her mother's free hand and placed it on her stomach. Sure enough, the baby was using the inside of her stomach for a punching bag.

Pam laughed and handed over the brownies. "I guess it's never too soon to start spoiling your grandchildren."

She stood up and went to the microwave to get the warmed-up stew. "Now that we've got the professor taken care of, so to speak, do you want to hear some good news?"

"By all means."

"You got another order for your toddler food from the Stork Store this morning. It's a good thing we put up so many bottles last month. Business is picking up, Missy."

Melissa nodded, happy her toddler-age baby food had found a local market. But her goal was to sell to the national grocery chains, and when that happened she'd have to move her manufacturing headquarters out of her mother's extra kitchen in the basement of her house and into a separate and appropriate building, as well as hire some actual employees. So far, she and her mother, father and brothers had been handling the business.

"Things are looking up, Missy," her mother announced as she set Melissa's stew on the counter and waved her over. "Now come and eat."

Melissa obeyed, but stole a glance at her mother's beaming and optimistic expression, wondering if she was entertaining hopes that had as much to do with Charles Avery as they did with Melissa's burgeoning business. If so, her mother needed to pull back on the reins. Melissa knew the danger of too many hopes, too much dreaming.

WHEN MELISSA ARRIVED at Charles's house the next morning, she was on time and wearing makeup. Her hair was down and flowing around her shoulders—pregnancy had at least been good for her hair and nails—and she'd worn one of her favorite yellow maternity blouses and white slacks. Apparently she was more foolish than she'd have ever imagined, because she was allowing her mother's encouraging words to influence her behavior in respect to Charles Avery.

But Charles barely looked at her as he bid her good morning, gave a quick rundown of his schedule for the day and left the house for Westminster College and his twice-a-week classes. He did mention, however, that he'd be home in time for her afternoon nap, so she should plan on it.

Melissa had barely mumbled a thank-you, which he didn't appear to hear, and then he was gone. If he'd had a crush on her in high school, as her mother had suggested, there was apparently no danger or sign of the old feelings reemerging.

Crestfallen but grateful for the reality check, Melissa turned to the children and immersed herself in caring for them. She *did* bake the cookies, though. After all, she *did* owe Charles for the tutoring thirteen years ago, and he *was* going over and above the usual duties of an employer by insisting she have afternoon naps.

The children enjoyed helping to make, then eating some of the cookies, and it took up most of the morning. They also colored in some coloring books she'd bought at a discount store last week, did toddler aerobics to a tape with one of their favorite puppet TV personalities, and listened while she read several books. She was hoping to have the kids tired out enough by the afternoon that they'd play quietly while Charles watched them during her nap.

Charles came home just before two o'clock, just as he'd promised. He was polite, but distant, and advised her to use Mrs. Butters's room for her nap.

"You can use the alarm clock she keeps by the bed, too," he offered as she turned to go. "Set it for three-fifteen, not three."

She must have looked puzzled, because he quickly explained, "In case you don't go to sleep right away. You need at least an hour or you won't be refreshed. Annette always said less than an hour just made her irritable when she got up, and more than an hour made her feel groggy the rest of the day."

Melissa thought about this and agreed. "I never thought about it before, but she was right." She tentatively smiled, but Charles was already walking away, down the hall.

Melissa mumbled, "Guess he's not going to wish me sweet dreams," and went directly to Mrs. Butters's room. Despite her anxiety about Charles's response to her cookies, and her disappointment over his suddenly distant attitude, Melissa was too tired to lie awake and worry about it. As soon as she'd set the alarm and her head hit the pillow, she was asleep.

CHARLES WAS READY to play with the kids and asked them what they wanted to do. They begged to watch a video and Charles agreed to it when he noticed that they were dragging a little and might even nap in front of the television if given half a chance. Mrs. Butters wouldn't approve, but what the heck. Daniel's thumb was in his mouth and Sarah was twirling her hair around her fingers, pre-sleep activities for both.

Once they were settled in the family room, Charles went to his study to put away his briefcase and quickly go over a few papers turned in by students that morning. He was enjoying the quietness of the house and not regretting in the least his decision to demand that Melissa nap every afternoon.

As he reached his desk, he noticed two baskets covered with clear wrapping paper and tied at the top with gold ribbon.

"What the—?"

Upon inspection, he saw that the baskets were filled to the brim with cookies...the cookies Melissa had promised to bake him for his kindness in allowing her to nap, obviously. But why two baskets? He shook his head, pleased but wishing he wasn't pleased. He had been impatient with and alarmed by his preoccupation with Missy's presence in the house yesterday, by his vivid recalling of his high-school crush, by his distraction and attraction. There, he'd admitted it. He was still powerfully attracted to her.

The baskets had little notes attached to them. He was ashamed of his eagerness as he opened the first, which read, *For the naps. Melissa.* And then the second, which read, *For saving my GPA in high school. Sorry I'm a little late with this batch. Missy.*

Charles was pleased and, yes, touched. She did remember after all and was trying to make amends for being thoughtless thirteen years ago. He was smiling down at the second note, feeling his insides melt like soft butter in the sun, when the doorbell sounded its Westminster chime and he heard quick, childish footsteps—probably Christopher's—heading for the door.

Charles put away the note and left the study. As he walked down the hall toward the front of the house, he could hear his sister Lily's voice and the clamor of her three children. So much for a quiet house! He always welcomed Lily's visits, but this one was ill-timed. He didn't want Melissa's nap disturbed.

"Charles! How's it going, bro?"

Lily's red hair hadn't softened to auburn as Charles's had. And she wore it in outrageous styles, such as her present "do," which framed her face in rakish angles like an exploding haystack. Her husband, Josh, called the style "Meg-Ryan-on-speed." But like Meg, Lily's impish face and outgoing personality allowed her to carry off hairdos and clothes that other women didn't dare try.

"It's goin' good, sis," Charles assured her in a lowered voice. His twin nephews, Matt and Mark, who were the same age as Daniel, and his niece, Amanda, who was Sarah's age, buzzed around him like bees around a hive. "But why don't we herd the kids into the family room and close the door? My nanny's taking a nap."

Lily looked incredulous. "Your nanny's taking a *nap?* So, who's watching the kids?"

"Well, I am. But it's just for an—"

"I told you, Charles, to let *me* take care of the kids this week. You were worried it would be too much for me, but *I* told you I could handle it. But, *no,* you had to hire temporary help and now she's taking advantage of your kindness and generosity. How are you going to get your lecture ready?"

"Lily, please lower your voice," Charles implored. "You're going to wake her." By now Sarah and Daniel had emerged from the family room and all six children were laughing and talking and running around the living room.

Lily shook her head. "Really, Charles, I don't understand this. Why does she need a nap? Is she elderly?"

"No. She's pregnant."

"Well, pregnancy does tire you out, but—"

"Especially in your last month," Charles pointed out. "She's nearly full-term, Lily. She really needs the rest or she's exhausted by dinnertime." He waved his hands over his head, trying to get the children's attention. "Want to watch a video in the family room, kids?"

"But what about your work?"

"I can still get it done. One hour every afternoon is not going to slow me down significantly."

"*Every* afternoon?" Lily shook her head again, obviously not ready to let the subject drop. "Doesn't she go home after dinner? She has all evening to recuperate. I don't mean to sound heartless, Charles, but you hired her to watch the kids. Lots of pregnant women work, but if she's too pregnant to do the job, then—"

"I'm sorry to interrupt. I heard the kids and thought maybe something was going on that required the assistance of your…er…nanny."

Charles turned to see Melissa standing just outside the living room, in the hall. Her hair was mussed and her eyes looked drowsily sexy. Her cheeks were flushed, whether from sleep or embarrassment, he couldn't know. Had she heard what Lily had been saying? He hoped not!

"Melissa, sorry we woke you," Charles said with an apologetic smile, determined to carry on as if she hadn't heard them. "My sister, Lily, came over with the kids."

While Sarah grabbed Melissa's leg and her attention momentarily, Lily leaned over and whispered to Charles, "Why didn't you tell me it was *her*. Now I understand, big bro."

MELISSA HAD BEEN jolted out of a deep sleep and she still felt a little disoriented. But not too disoriented to have heard Lily arguing with Charles as she walked down the hall toward the living room. Apparently Charles's little sister thought Melissa was not up to the job of being nanny to her niece and nephews. What troubled Melissa most was the depressing possibility that Lily might be right.

"Did you two know each other in high school?" Charles asked uncomfortably.

"Everyone knew who Melissa Richardson was," Lily answered, trying to look and sound friendly, but only managing a strained facsimile. "But I wouldn't say we actually *knew* each other. Boy...I haven't seen you since high school. You haven't changed a bit...well, except for—" She gestured vaguely toward Melissa's pregnant belly.

"I haven't seen you, either," Melissa offered, trying for the same friendly tone and sounding just as strained as Lily. "Although I don't suppose we saw much of each other while we were in high school, anyway. It was a big school, and aren't you three years younger than me?"

"Nope. I was just two years behind you. I was a sophomore when you were a senior…and the head cheerleader and Homecoming Queen."

By the way she was looking her over, Melissa could swear Lily was surprised she wasn't holding pom-poms and wearing a tiara. "Well, that was a long time ago."

"And now you're pregnant," Lily finished, too brightly. "Your first?"

"Yes." *Please don't ask about Brad. Please, please, please…*

"And how's Brad? What is he, a bank president or something by now? Or the world's greatest shoe salesman? That guy could win over anyone with his charm." Warming to the subject, she smiled and continued. "I remember once, he—"

"Lily, could I talk to you in the kitchen for a moment?" Charles interrupted.

Lily was clearly confused, but agreed. "Sure. Okay. But should we leave Melissa with all these rambunctious kids?"

Melissa felt her defenses rising. "I think I can manage them for a couple of minutes by myself," she said stiffly.

"Oh, okay." Lily looked distressed, as if realizing for a fact that Melissa had heard her talking with Charles, adamantly pointing out that a nearly nine-months-pregnant woman who needed a nap every afternoon wasn't a fit nanny. Melissa hated to admit it, but Lily was right. She might as well face the truth. She'd offer her resignation as soon as Lily left and she and Charles had a moment alone.

"Lily, my God, what have you done? I think she heard you."

"I *know* she heard me, Charles. I'm sorry. I didn't know your nanny was Melissa Richardson or I would have kept my trap shut."

"What's that got to do with it?" Charles asked her, flustered and defensive. "I hope I would have shown the same consideration for any pregnant woman who came to my house to watch my kids."

"I still think she's too pregnant for the job, and you probably think the same thing, Charles. Admit it! But because it's the girl you regularly swooned over for at least your entire senior year, I don't blame you for making allowances."

"For your information, little sister, Melissa is one helluva nanny. If she wasn't pregnant and didn't have to bring it down a notch, she'd be stiff competition for Mary Poppins. The kids love her. I—"

"Love her?" Lily teased, obviously beginning to enjoy her brother's discomfort.

"I respect and admire her, particularly given the fact that she's about to have a baby and is doing it all by herself."

Lily's eyes widened. "She's divorced? Ol' Brad flew the coop?"

"No, Lily. She's a widow."

This fact finally shut Lily up. Her brows furrowed, her eyes filled with sympathy. "Oh, Charles. I'm really sorry. I'll bet she actually needs this job, huh? What a dumbbell I am!"

"Forget it," Charles said, his displeasure dissipating at the obvious remorse Lily felt. "But I want you to understand that I'm not keeping Melissa on as nanny because I pity her, or any such nonsense.

She's here because she's doing a great job. I was the one who made her promise to take a daily nap. I made it a requirement. It'll get her through the afternoon and safely home without me worrying about her falling asleep at the wheel.''

"Okay, I believe you," Lily conceded, holding up both hands. "She's a great nanny! But I still think you're smitten, Charles. She's still just as pretty as she was in high school." She leaned forward and whispered, "And now she's *available.*"

MELISSA SOMEHOW MANAGED to get through Lily's short visit, then the rest of the long day, even though she was more tired than usual because of her interrupted nap. She was also depressed because she was going to tell Charles to request another nanny from the agency. To make matters worse, the children were especially engaging and wonderful to be around that afternoon. She'd only known them two days, and she was already going to miss them.

She made sure she didn't show how tired she was and fixed dinner and cleared up afterward with all the appearance of cheerfulness and energy. But it took everything in her to fake it convincingly... especially with Charles watching her so closely. She couldn't read his expression, though. She had no idea what he was thinking. Maybe he'd be relieved when she told him she was quitting. Maybe he'd be glad to see her go.

"Can I talk to you before I go home, Charles?" Melissa requested as she sponged off the counter in the kitchen. He was just going past the door with Daniel under his arm like a football. He'd given all three children baths after dinner and was headed for the bedroom to read them a bedtime story.

"Sure. I wanted to talk to you, anyway." He tickled Daniel under the arm. "Did you say good-night to Melissa, Daniel?"

Daniel giggled uncontrollably, as his father continued to tickle him. "What's the matter, Daniel? Cat got your tongue? Why can't you say good-night to Melissa? Huh? Huh?"

Daniel gasped and giggled and tried to get the words out, his face aglow with merriment.

"It's all right, Daniel," Melissa finally said, laughing. "I know you want to say good-night, but your dad's making it impossible. Sweet dreams, sweetie." *And goodbye,* she finished sadly to herself.

"Can you wait till I'm through reading to them?" Charles asked her. "It'll only take a few minutes."

"Sure," Melissa answered. What were a few more minutes? "I'll wait for you in the family room. I have some of the kids' clothes to fold, anyway."

"I'll see you soon, then."

IT TOOK Charles a little longer than he expected to finish the book the children particularly wanted him to read that night. When he was finally done reading the last page and the kids were fighting to keep their eyes open, he kissed them good-night, turned off the light and left the room. Sarah had a room of her own, but he didn't want to risk waking her up by carrying her to her own bed. She could sleep with Daniel for one night. It was too important to talk to Melissa and get everything straightened out.

Charles didn't go directly to the family room. And he didn't question his motives when he took a side trip to his bedroom and spiffed himself up in the master bathroom. With freshly brushed teeth and combed hair, he finally headed toward the family room. He was eager to thank Melissa for the cookies, and to smooth over whatever hurt feelings she might have because of the opinions Lily had expressed a little too loudly earlier that day.

But that was Lily for you. She always had good intentions, but not always the best manner in handling them. Lily's concern that Charles might be saddled with an inadequate nanny was just her being overprotective of him and the kids. It was her nature to be bossy and a little overzealous at times. He hoped Melissa would understand.

"Sorry it took me so long—" But Charles's words were wasted. Melissa was lying on the sofa, surrounded by neatly folded laundry, fast asleep.

Chapter Four

Melissa's palms, pressed together prayerlike, were tucked under her cheek. She looked adorable...and exhausted. Charles wasn't about to wake her up for a talk, or to send her home, for that matter. He went to the linen closet, found a light blanket, covered her up, then turned off the light. He made sure the night-light was on in the hall in case she woke up and wasn't sure where she was, or needed to go to the bathroom.

Then he looked up the phone number of Melissa's parents. Fortunately, because they hadn't moved since he'd tutored Melissa thirteen years ago, it was easy to find.

He punched in the numbers and waited for an answer.

"Hello?"

"Mrs. Richardson?"

"Yes?" answered a voice he vaguely remembered.

"This is Charles Avery."

There was a pause, then an "Oh!" That was all she said, just "Oh!" He wasn't sure if she even knew who he was, so he continued.

"I don't know if you knew, but Melissa's been working for me as a nanny this week."

"Yes, she told me." Her tone suddenly changed. "She's all right, isn't she?"

"She's fine," Charles quickly assured her. "It's just that she's fallen asleep on my sofa in the family room and I don't want to wake her. I was afraid you might call her place, and when she didn't answer, worry. It's only eight o'clock, but she might just sleep through the night if I don't disturb her. She's worked real hard these last two days, and I know she's dead-tired. You don't think she'll mind my letting her sleep here all night, do you?"

"I don't know if she'll mind or not, Charles," Mrs. Richardson answered with a definite note of warmth in her voice, "but I totally approve of what you're doing. It's good to know someone's watching out for her. But then you helped her out in high school, too, didn't you?"

Charles was surprised that Mrs. Richardson remembered and even mentioned those three weeks of tutoring. "Well, it was no big deal."

"It was to Missy. You saved her GPA. She got that scholarship to the University of Utah she wanted, so she could attend the same school as Brad." Mrs. Richardson sighed. "Too bad she was never able to use it. She was too busy supporting Brad—his football scholarship didn't quite cover all his expenses, you know—and doing most of *his* classwork."

Charles couldn't think of an appropriate or polite response to this statement, so he said nothing. But he was busy taking in everything Mrs. Richardson had said.

So, Missy had continued doing for Brad in college what she'd done for him in high school...

This revelation made Charles angry. Angrier than he had any right to be, particularly given the fact that Brad was dead and couldn't defend himself against Mrs. Richardson's implied criticism, or Charles's own inclination to continue to think ill of him. It made Charles a little angry with Melissa, too. He wondered how long she had allowed Brad to take advantage of her like that. But he wasn't going to ask her mother.

"I suppose Melissa told you about Brad? Explained that he's not...you know..."

Her voice trailed off, as if hoping he'd finish her sentence. Perhaps Melissa's mother was just as averse to plain-speaking about Brad's death as Melissa was.

"That he's not...with us any longer?" Charles finished for her, hoping he'd chosen the euphemism she'd apparently been struggling for.

He heard her sigh again. Despite her earlier disparaging comment, it appeared as though she missed Brad, too. That had definitely been a *pensive* sigh.

"Yes...well, thanks again for calling, Charles."

"Just didn't want you to worry, Mrs. Richardson."

"Oh please, Charles, call me Pam."

Charles wasn't sure if they'd ever speak again, but readily agreed to call her by her first name. "All right, Pam."

"Better sleep light tonight, Charles, 'cause Melissa might wake up at 2:00 a.m. and decide to drive home," was Pam's parting advice. "She's funny like that. Doesn't want to be perceived as falling short on

the job. But I don't think it would be a good idea
for her to drive alone at that hour and in her condition.''

Charles agreed and told her so. He intended to
sleep light, listening as usual for his three children—
and now his nanny.

In his study, he worked on his paper till midnight,
keeping the door open. On the way to bed, he
checked on Melissa, found her lying on her back with
one arm and hand resting on her stomach, and the
other arm arced over her head. The expression on her
face was more rested, more peaceful than before.

Charles smiled with satisfaction. He'd done the
right thing, letting her sleep. He continued on down
the hall, checked on the kids, then quickly got ready
for bed with the doors to both his bedroom and his
bathroom open. He slipped under the cool sheets and
drifted to sleep, wondering about all the things that
must have happened to Melissa since high school.
They hadn't had a chance, really, to talk and get
reacquainted.

Did she finally go to college?

Did Brad ever grow up and behave like an adult,
taking responsibility for his own classwork and financial support?

Unfortunately, it would be pretty difficult getting
answers to these questions without being a little bit
nosy and, more importantly, without mentioning
Brad. And Melissa had expressly asked Charles *not*
to mention Brad.

WHEN MELISSA woke up, she was completely confused. Although morning light flooded the room, she
didn't recognize her surroundings. Where the heck

was she? More urgently, *where was the bathroom?* She had to go *bad.* A baby on her bladder did not make holding it in very easy...or wise.

She sat up, blinked several times, then realized where she was. It was the family room at Charles's house. Yes, she could hear him and the children in the kitchen. She could smell breakfast smells. She must have fallen asleep on the sofa, folding clothes while she waited to talk to Charles!

Now she remembered everything. She had been going to tell Charles she was quitting, that he should call Nanny on the Spot first thing in the morning and demand another nanny. One who wasn't pregnant.

Melissa searched the room for a clock. The VCR was actually programmed to show the correct time— well, after all, Charles was a brilliant science professor and ought to be able to program just about anything—and it was...*nine-thirty!* "First thing in the morning" had come and gone! Despite the agency's name, he'd be lucky to get a nanny today, much less on the spot, even if he had the added claim of needing to replace a nanny who wasn't up to snuff, so to speak.

Melissa struggled to her feet. Now that she was no longer horizontal, she needed to go to the bathroom worse than ever! Running was an awkward business in one's final few days of pregnancy, but Melissa felt she had no choice.

As she reached the door, who should show up, of course, but Charles. "You're awake," he began cheerfully. "Did you—?"

But Melissa didn't dare wait to chitchat with Charles. She barely squeezed past him in the doorway—*barely* being the operative word—her full

breasts and belly grazing his hard chest and flat ab-
domen in the process. She was glad none of the kids
showed up in the hallway, or they might have been
in danger of being mowed down by an out-of-control
pregnant lady on a beeline to the bathroom.

In a couple of minutes, Melissa was feeling much
better...until she caught a glimpse of herself in the
mirror as she was washing her hands! The mascara
she'd applied so carefully yesterday was now dark
smudges under her eyes. The corduroy-covered sofa
pillow she'd found too comfortable to resist resting
her head on the night before had left an indented
pattern of lines on her right cheek. She must not have
moved for hours to get such a permanent-looking
tattoo! Her hair hung listlessly around her face, and
she definitely needed some lipstick. Not to mention
a toothbrush and a nice, hot shower.

Oh, how was she going to get through this day
looking and feeling so dreadful? But even as Melissa
continued to gaze, dismayed, at her appearance, she
knew she wasn't going to let Charles down. He'd let
her sleep out of consideration for her, and she wasn't
going to run off to her apartment to clean up and
make herself feel more presentable. She'd already
made him waste half his morning, doing all the
things *she* was supposed to be doing.

The children were probably about finished eating.
They'd need help dressing, then she'd have to clean
up the breakfast dishes, plan lunch and dinner, and
get the kids started on some fun activity.

And Charles—dear, sweet, considerate Charles—
needed to get his paper done for the conference this
weekend!

Steeling her resolve, Melissa found a comb in a

drawer, yanked it quickly through her hair till her eyes watered and her hair was snarl-free and smooth, then tied up a ponytail with one of Sarah's ribbons. Never mind that the style was extremely severe, she didn't have time to shampoo.

She turned on the water full-bore and washed her face, scrubbing away at the smudges under her eyes, then patted her cheeks dry. Damn...that ribbed pattern on her cheek was still there. And it didn't look like it was going anywhere anytime soon. Sighing, she found some mouthwash and rinsed thoroughly.

Feeling marginally better, but looking as plain Jane as possible, Melissa left the bathroom and walked down the hall toward the kitchen. That's when she noticed how wrinkled her favorite yellow blouse was, the one she'd chosen so carefully yesterday. But what did she expect? She'd slept in it!

She heard Charles talking, chuckling. And some other voice...a woman's voice. Was Lily there again?

Melissa was already embarrassed. Embarrassed by her appearance. Embarrassed by the way she'd hurried past Charles to the bathroom. Embarrassed by the physical contact they'd made while she'd squeezed past him through the doorway.

She expected to feel even more embarrassed when she first met Charles's eyes. Lily's, too. *Especially* Lily's, because by passing out on the sofa and spending the night, Melissa had again proven she was too pregnant to do the job. But she lifted her chin and kept walking toward the kitchen because she'd already made up her mind to quit at the end of the day, and she'd tell Lily just that!

What Melissa *hadn't* expected when she reached

the kitchen was to actually want a hole to open up in the earth and swallow her. But then it was a bit of a surprise to find Charles at the sink, rinsing dishes, while two gorgeous young women looked on. One of them—an exotic-looking girl with long, glossy black hair—had propped her lithe body in a languid pose against the refrigerator. She was wearing a tiny white T-shirt—braless—and a pair of hip-hugger jeans that showed off her flat, tanned belly and her long, *long* legs.

The other one—a voluptuous blonde à la Britney Spears—leaned over the dining bar, her fists supporting her chin as she gazed up at Charles adoringly, all the while revealing a great deal of cleavage at the top of her low-cut, midriff-baring blouse.

Melissa didn't think either of them could be more than twenty.

Charles seemed unfazed by the attention, his hands never pausing as he slipped the dishes under the running tap water, scrubbing away maple syrup and bits of waffle before bending to place them in the dishwasher. At the same time, he was talking away enthusiastically about some meteor shower that was supposed to appear that night. The two girls—apparently college students—were spellbound by everything he was saying, and especially by the view of his very fine behind as he bent to put things in the dishwasher.

The children were nowhere in sight.

So far Melissa hadn't been sighted, either, and she didn't intend to be. She'd slink off and find the children, with whom she felt fairly sure of not feeling horribly embarrassed and lacking.

Too late.

"Melissa."

It was more a statement than a greeting. Charles had caught sight of her. There was a smile on his lips, which slowly slipped away as he studied her face. Either he could see she was mortified, or he could see and understand *why* she was mortified, or both.

The blonde and the brunette both turned and looked at her. Neither of them appeared inclined to be critical, but then why should they waste their time being critical of or—hah!—jealous of a frumpy nanny?

"Oh, you must be Mrs. Butters," the blonde said. "The professor has told us about you."

"Only he never said you were pregnant," the beautiful brunette added, sliding her long slim fingers over her own flat belly in an unconscious gesture of empathy...or thankfulness. "I thought you were too old to *get* pregnant."

"Don't be silly, Kimberly," the blonde said. "Obviously the professor lied about his nanny's age." She smiled ingenuously at Melissa. "You're not a day over forty, are you, Mrs. Butters? And even if you were, lots of women these days have babies in their forties."

The brunette frowned, assessing Melissa again. "I expected you to look a lot more motherly. Mrs. Butters is such a *motherly* name. Kind of like Mrs. Potts in *Beauty and the Beast,* you know? Plump and—"

Charles had been trying to interrupt from the beginning, but there had been no pauses in the girls' conversation. "She's not Mrs. Butters," he was finally able to interject. "This is Melissa, our temporary nanny."

"Oh," they said in unison.

"Pleased to meet you," said the blonde. "I'm Tiffany."

"Yes, nice to meet you," the brunette echoed politely. "I'm Kimberly."

"Nice to meet you, too," Melissa mumbled, managing a strained smile. She was painfully aware of her disheveled appearance and eager to make a quick exit. "I was looking for the children, but I can see they're not in here, so—"

"They're in the family room," Charles said. "I told them to wait for you in there. I gave Christopher permission to put in a video since I wasn't sure how long it would take you to—"

Charles abruptly ended his sentence. He was probably going to say he wasn't sure how long it would take her to "freshen up." Obviously he could see she hadn't taken nearly long enough. But if she took the time she needed, she'd be taking advantage of Charles again. *No way.* The clock was ticking and he was paying for every minute.

"Okay. Thanks," Melissa said finally, and quickly left the room. As she hurried down the hall toward the family room, she could feel the tears welling in her eyes again. She couldn't blame this particular burst of emotion on her pregnancy hormones, either. She knew very well she was comparing herself to the two college students and feeling old and fat and really stupid for thinking Charles might be interested in her when he could obviously have his pick from a bevy of hot young college women. At thirty-one, he really wasn't that much older than they were, either. It wouldn't be like robbing the cradle.

Before entering the family room, she wiped away

her tears and put on a bright smile. Like Charles, the children deserved the best nanny she could be.

AFTER KIMBERLY and Tiffany left, Charles quickly went to his study and called Lily.

"Lil? What are you doing?"

"Why, bro? What's wrong?"

"I need your help. Melissa spent the night here and—"

"*What?* Hey, Charles, aren't you going a little fast with Miss Homecoming Queen?"

"It wasn't like that, Lily. She fell asleep on the sofa in the family room. She looked so peaceful, and I knew how tired she must be, so I didn't wake her up. She slept till nine-thirty this morning and I think she's embarrassed."

"Yeah, well, I'm sure she is. Especially after hearing my little diatribe yesterday."

"I'm sure she's anxious to get busy right away and try to make up for lost time and all that, but I thought she'd at least take a couple of minutes to shower. Get the kinks out after sleeping on the sofa."

"She didn't, I gather."

"No, and when she came out of the bathroom, looking for the kids, she saw me in the kitchen with a couple of college students and—"

"Girls, of course," Lily stated drily. "Nubile little wenches in crop tops and tight jeans, I suppose."

"They were just—"

"No need to answer. I've seen some of your groupies."

"They're not groupies."

"No, I'm sure they're serious science students," Lily said with a sniff.

"Listen, Lily, they just came by to ask me what time the meteor shower would be visible tonight."

"Whatever," Lily said dismissively. "The bottom line is, at nearly nine months pregnant, Melissa is already feeling awkward and unattractive."

"I think pregnant women are beautiful," Charles protested. "Annette never looked more beautiful to me than when she was ready to give birth."

"I'm sure Annette appreciated that about you, Charles, but I would bet my life that, on some days, she felt less than sexy."

Charles knew this was true. There were days when Annette was pregnant that it took everything in his power to convince her he still found her sexy and attractive. But he certainly hadn't minded the convincing part...

When Charles said nothing, Lily continued. "Facing those two college students, all primped up to impress you, was probably pretty devastating to Melissa, especially since she'd had no shower, was wearing no makeup, and was forced to wear clothes she'd slept in overnight."

"She just looked a little bed-rumpled to me," Charles said. *And sexy,* he added to himself. "And she looks great without makeup. She has natural beauty."

"But you didn't tell her that, I suppose?"

"I didn't exactly have the opportunity with my students in the room, but I wouldn't have said anything anyway. She'd probably think I was coming on to her, or just placating her."

"So, the reason you called me was—?"

"To ask you to come over and relieve her for a

while so she can take a shower, iron her blouse, whatever it takes for her to feel better.''

''Are you sure I'm the person to do this?'' Lily asked cautiously. ''She already thinks I don't approve of her doing the nanny thing. Me coming over might just embarrass her further.''

''Who else am I going to ask, Lily? I don't think her pride would tolerate *me* insisting she take a bath and freshen up, do you? Besides, you're the ideal person for this job. You're bossy by nature. She might not be able to refuse anything you ask...or order. Just come on over and do your best.''

''Okay,'' Lily finally agreed. ''The kids and I will be over in a few minutes.''

Charles hung up the phone, glad he could count on his intrepid little sister during times of crisis. He smiled and shook his head ruefully. He'd never imagined he'd consider the preservation of Missy Richardson's personal comfort and peace of mind a crisis situation. But somehow, it had become important to him.

MELISSA HAD JUST gotten the kids dressed and was discussing possibilities with them about how they could spend their day when the doorbell rang. Christopher ran out of the room to answer it. His father allowed him to answer the door, but always followed right behind him.

Dreading the possibility that it might be a couple more Gap-commercial babes from the college, Melissa was tempted to allow Christopher to handle whoever was there. Unless the doorbell-ringer was a kidnapper or some other nefarious person, she knew he'd do just fine. But it would be irresponsible to allow a four-year-old to answer the door unsupervised, and she didn't want to put Christopher at risk just to avoid embarrassing herself again, so Melissa followed him into the living-room.

Melissa's heart sank when she saw it was Lily again, with all three of her children.

"Hi, Christopher. Hi, Melissa," Lily called cheerfully as she entered the room. "Don't worry, I don't drop by every day," she added, possibly responding to the dismayed expression on Melissa's face, an expression she was trying valiantly to hide.

"I just thought I'd offer to take the kids to the park and give you a little free time to do…oh, I don't know…whatever!" She leaned close to Melissa and whispered, "Have you seen Charles's whirlpool tub in the master bathroom? When Annette was pregnant, she climbed in that tub every chance she got. Of course, she always made sure the water was lukewarm, not hot. Hot water's not good for pregnant women, but I'm sure you already knew that. Soaking in the jetted tub really helped her relax, and, frankly, Melissa, you look like you could use a half hour or so of total relaxation. What did ya do, girl? Sleep here last night?"

So far, Melissa hadn't had a chance to utter a single word of greeting, or anything else for that matter. Lily had come in like a walking, talking whirling dervish and given Melissa no chance to speak. Now that Lily had wound down, Melissa couldn't speak because there was a giant lump in her throat. And those damn tears were welling up again!

"Charles called you, didn't he?" Melissa finally asked her, her voice embarrassingly raspy from emotion. "Don't deny it, Lily. This operation has his fingerprints all over it."

Lily smiled understandingly. "Sure, he called me. He told me you fell asleep on the sofa last night, and—"

"Which only confirms what you were saying yesterday. That I'm unfit to—"

"Forget what I said. I was just concerned about Charles and the kids, but he assures me that you're nothing short of a Mary Poppins. So what if you need some rest? Sounds like with all you do, even if you weren't pregnant you'd need an afternoon nap!"

One tear skittered out of the corner of her eye and Melissa quickly dashed it away. "You're being very kind."

"No, Charles is being kind. This was his idea, remember? Now just let him have his way, okay? Besides, if I blow this, he'll kill me! I can take the kids to the park for an hour, and by the time I come back you'll feel like a new woman. Trust me, that whirlpool tub is to die for."

"But isn't it too hot to go to the park?"

"Not for another couple of hours. Besides, if it starts heating up, we'll duck into an ice cream parlor or get some cold drinks."

Melissa bit her lip. She could feel herself caving. She could imagine herself in the whirlpool tub, an indulgence she hadn't enjoyed since her honeymoon with Brad at a lodge in Sun Valley, Idaho. "Are you sure you can handle all six of them at once?"

"Now who's doubting who?" Lily teased. "I've done it a million times. I have a bark like a drill sergeant and the kids fall in line the minute I use it."

"But about the whirlpool tub... Are you sure Charles won't mind if I use it?"

"He suggested it himself."

"Well, okay. Thanks, Lily," Melissa finally said with a grateful smile. "I know I'll feel much better once I've cleaned up."

Lily reached into her purse and pulled out a toothbrush, still in its packaging, and a tube of lipstick. "These might help, too. Although Charles says you have natural beauty, most women feel better with a bit of lipstick on."

With Melissa's help, it took Lily less than ten minutes to corral, dress and belt the children into her minivan. Melissa felt a little bemused as she watched them drive away, but part of her dazed state might have had something to do with Lily's offhand comment that Charles thought she had "natural beauty."

When Melissa went back inside, she tiptoed down the hall and peeked around a corner to get a look at the door to Charles's study. If it was open, she'd go in and thank him for his kindness and then offer to resign at the end of the day. If it was closed, she'd wait till lunchtime to interrupt him.

It was closed. A little relieved to be putting off the resignation speech, et cetera, she went directly to the linen closet and retrieved two large, fluffy towels for her bath.

Melissa felt strange invading Charles's bedroom. But he'd told Lily it was okay for her to use the tub, and the only way to get to the master bathroom was through the bedroom, so she wasn't really trespassing. But it sure felt that way. It was also a little intriguing and provocative, the idea of seeing the bed where he slept, the room where he relaxed and changed clothes.

It was a large room and had a definite masculine flavor in the solid furniture and tailored bedspread and drapes. The colors were burgundy and gray. Melissa decided he must have redecorated since Annette's death, which he might have done to help him get on with his life. His wife's personal touches and possessions were probably the most poignant reminders of his loss, and he'd have had to part with them eventually, or store them away, in order to get on with his life.

Ah, but he still kept her picture on his dresser! It was the first and only picture of Annette that Melissa had seen in the house. Clutching the thick towels to her chest, she crept timidly toward the picture, curious and guilt-ridden. It was so wrong of her to have claimed Brad was dead when this poor woman had actually passed on, leaving behind such a sweet, young, promising family!

Melissa could see the resemblance between Annette and Sarah immediately. Annette had been a brunette, her hair thick and wavy and falling to her shoulders. She had large, soft brown eyes and a wonderful smile. No wonder she and Charles had such beautiful children.

As she stared at the portrait, Melissa promised herself that she'd tell Charles the truth about Brad. Before she left his house for good, she'd tell him everything. She owed him—and Annette—at least that.

Having made this promise to herself, Melissa went into the bathroom with a clearer conscience and a happier anticipation of the delights of a whirlpool tub. In a few minutes, she was deeply immersed in lukewarm, swirling water, her towel-wrapped head propped against the rim of the tub, her eyes closed. She'd already washed her hair and scrubbed herself clean, and now that her grungy feeling was gone, she could feel her muscles relaxing, her nerves soothing. She even found herself doing a little sexy fantasizing.

It had certainly been a long time since she'd felt sexy, or even had sexy thoughts that lasted more than a millisecond. Normally she would subdue such thoughts, but she was actually *nurturing* them. It was as if she was starting to believe that someday she might be able to love again…and be loved in return. To desire someone…and be desired.

How much of this new attitude and optimism had something to do with the kind and considerate way Charles treated her? she wondered. Or the way she sometimes caught him looking at her?

Of course, the star of Melissa's little mind-movie was none other than Charles. Yes, the professor made a perfectly wonderful hero for her fantasy. Not only was he handsome, sexy, intelligent, kind and well-to-do, he was a good father. And when one was as large with child as she was, even a fantasy hero had to be a good father before he could be allowed in her imagination to kiss, caress and…er…otherwise romance her.

Melissa had taken her fantasy to rather daring lengths when she suddenly realized that the water was cooling. She'd been in the tub a half hour! She certainly didn't want to be in the tub when Lily returned with the children! And she still had to dry her hair and iron her blouse.

Melissa nudged down the little drain lever with her toe, then carefully pushed herself up and out of the water. She just as carefully stepped out onto the bath-mat and dried herself off. Her day-old clothes were draped over the hamper, but she was reluctant to put them on again after the bath had left her feeling so clean and refreshed. Besides, what was she going to wear for a top while she ironed her blouse?

That's when Melissa saw Charles's robe hanging on a hook on the closed bathroom door. At least she assumed it was Charles's robe. It was burgundy and looked very soft and inviting... Surely Charles wouldn't mind if she wore it for a few minutes while she made her own clothes fit for wearing.

As she reached for Charles's robe, Melissa told herself that she wasn't at all intrigued by the inti-macy of wearing something against her skin that had been next to his. That wasn't why she was doing this. *Really*. She just needed to borrow a robe—*anyone's* robe.

She slipped her arms into the sleeves and felt the soft silk of the material slide sensuously over her nakedness, and she imagined Charles's hands doing the same thing...well, that was just a fleeting thought, she told herself, a leftover from the silly fantasizing she'd been doing in the tub.

However, when she took the long belt and tied it loosely around her middle, capturing and keeping the warmth of her just-bathed body inside the robe, she immediately drifted into another fantasy of being in Charles's arms, sharing passionate kisses, the two of them drifting down onto the bed.... That's when she knew she was out of control!

Impatient with her silly daydreaming, Melissa gave her reflection in the mirror a stern finger-wagging, straightened her towel-turban, abruptly grabbed her wrinkled clothes off the hamper, and flung open the bathroom door with new resolve. No more fantasizing! But she'd only made it halfway across the room and was still several feet from the bedroom door when Charles—the sexy superstar of her mental movie—suddenly walked in, apparently enjoying a bite of the half-eaten apple he held in his right hand.

When he saw her he stopped in his tracks, stopped chewing, and simply stared. On his handsome face was an expression of complete astonishment.

Astonishment…and something else.

Chapter Five

Charles had been on his way back to the study after raiding the kitchen for a mid-morning snack when he'd taken a detour to his bedroom to pick up the research book he'd left on his bedside table. He had assumed that Melissa used Mrs. Butters's bathroom for her shower, so he was completely surprised to find her in his bedroom.

In his robe.

All pink and rosy.

Smelling warm and steamy from her bath.

The bath she'd taken in *his* tub.

He couldn't help it. His gaze wandered. From the tip of her turbaned head, to her flushed cheeks and bright, startled eyes. From her slender neck, to the V of his robe where a little cleavage showed. But wasn't the robe warm enough? Her nipples were quite obvious where the fabric pulled snug across the front of her.

He swallowed hard and politely averted his gaze, but soon found himself confronted with another of Melissa's charms. One of her long, lovely legs was revealed, from mid-thigh to ankle, through a slit where the robe had fallen open in the front. He remembered watching those curvy, slender legs during high school football games. Kicking, climbing, splitting, jumping.

Ah, hell... Even her pregnant belly was sexy. Or maybe he should say, *especially* her pregnant belly was sexy. He felt a primal urge to take her into his arms. To protect her. To make love to her. To *claim* her as his. To claim that baby as his. God, how stupid was that? And how stupid did he look, standing there with caveman thoughts running rampant through his so-called civilized cerebrum?

Talk, Charles, he ordered. *Open your mouth and speak.*

"Melissa, I'm sorry. I didn't know you were using this bathroom."

Melissa looked stricken, embarrassed as hell. "Lily told me I could. I'm sorry. I thought you knew!"

"It doesn't matter. You're perfectly welcome to use it any time you get the urge—" *Charles, old boy, don't even mention the word.*

He tried again. "That is, I mean—"

Melissa tugged at the front of the robe, closing up any gaps, hiding every inch of pretty pink skin. "Charles, we need to talk."

Charles thought they *were* talking. And it was a pretty damn amazing thing that either of them were getting words out at all, given the circumstances. *He* was even having trouble breathing.

"I...I can't continue to take advantage of you like this," Melissa quickly continued. "You need to call the agency and have them send you another nanny tomorrow. Your sister is right. I'm too pregnant for this job. I fall asleep on your sofa, don't wake up till nine-thirty, then spend the rest of the morning trying to pull myself together while you and Lily do my job for me.''

Charles could see Melissa was dead serious. Her words were heartfelt. There were tears gathering in her eyes.

''Melissa, what are you talking about?'' he said with a smile and a gently admonishing shake of his head. ''You're a great nanny. You're doing a great job. The kids love you.''

Melissa shrugged her shoulders. ''Well, I love them, too,'' she said miserably.

Touched by this quick affection for his children, now Charles wanted more than ever to take her into his arms. To comfort her. To reassure her. To kiss every inch of that beautiful face. But since he couldn't do that, he had no choice but to resort to talking again.

''You only fell asleep last night because your nap was interrupted yesterday,'' he said. ''That's not going to happen again.''

The corner of her mouth lifted in a rueful smile. ''What? Fall asleep on the sofa or have my nap interrupted? I doubt you can guarantee either. I know *I* can't.''

Encouraged by her smile and wry humor, Charles took two steps and was now standing close enough to touch her. She was looking down, so he cupped her jaw with his hand and tilted her chin up, compelling her to look at him. ''Don't take my sister's little rant yesterday too much to heart. She just worries about me and the kids and sometimes gets carried away. We've talked since then and I told her how great you are and how hard you work. She's okay with you being here, and I—'' She blinked and that brief flutter of long lashes was just enough to distract him. *Damn*, who knew she'd be even prettier up close?

''And you?'' she prompted him in a whisper.

''And I—''

He broke off again, lost again in the thrill of standing so close, with the sensation of her soft warm cheek cradled in the palm of his hand, with the clean, sweet scent of her, with the uncertain, vulnerable expression in her beautiful blue eyes.

''I'm okay with it, too,'' he finished, deciding to be wise instead of impetuous. He let his hand drop and stepped back to a safer distance. His attraction to her was making him want to say things, express feelings he couldn't possibly be feeling after only three days in her company. She'd think he was coming on to her. Maybe he would be... She was the first woman he'd been attracted to since Annette's death. There had been a few dates, a few kisses, but nothing coming close to this.

Melissa didn't say anything. She just stood there and watched him with a little furrow between her brows, her hands, balled into fists, jammed into the pockets of his robe. Obviously his being ''okay'' with her staying on wasn't exactly the ringing endorsement she needed. And he couldn't blame her for that.

''I *want* you to stay, Melissa. Very much. But only if *you* want to. If it's too much for you, I completely understand. Only you can judge how much is too much, though, so I'm leaving the decision up to you. Your health and the health of the baby is the most important issue to consider here." He smiled warmly. "Have I finally made myself clear?"

She smiled back. "I think so. And I've always known you put my health and the baby's health first. It's considerate of you, but you've got to get your work done, too. I don't want to take advantage of you."

Oh, if only you would.

He cleared his throat. "You aren't. So…are you staying?"

She nodded her head, looking pleased and relieved. "Yes. Yes, I'll stay if you really want me to. If you really think I'm doing a good job despite my propensity to fall asleep on your sofa."

"Oh, I do," he again assured her, but his thoughts had drifted away to the sleeping on the sofa part and remembering how sweet and sexy she'd looked curled up in the midst of stacks of folded laundry.

"Okay, but I've got to get dressed right away. I feel so much better and I've got lots to do! Besides, I don't want to be caught standing here in your robe when the children get home."

"Especially by Lily," he teased.

"Yes, especially by Lily," she agreed with a chuckle. "Although Christopher would probably have the most questions and be the most persistent in asking them! But this is really Lily's fault, you know. She told me you actually suggested I use the whirlpool tub. Implied that you might even be angry with her if she failed to convince me to use it." She breezed past him, headed for the door, one hand clutching the front of the robe, the other keeping her turban from falling off. "She must have got her wires crossed somehow."

Charles nodded in agreement, but couldn't agree less. Lily rarely got her wires crossed. He suspected she'd urged Melissa to use the tub on purpose. Perhaps she'd hoped to put Charles and Melissa in just the sort of predicament in which they'd found themselves.

Charles watched Melissa hurry down the hall, her cute behind wiggling under the fabric of his robe…which he might never wash again. Then he remembered the cookies.

"Missy?"

She turned, her hands still clutching the robe and securing the turban. "Yes?"

"Thanks for the cookies."

She smiled. "Just a little overdue," she admitted ruefully, then turned the corner and was gone.

"But well worth the wait," Charles murmured to himself.

WHEN LILY RETURNED with the children, they'd had lunch and tons of exercise. They were ready to settle down to quiet activities for the remainder of the day. And Melissa was more than ready for them. Her blouse was freshly ironed, her hair blown dry and styled, her teeth brushed, her lips colored and glossed, and even her lashes curled and coated with mascara—thanks to a raid on the makeup drawer in Mrs. Butters's bathroom. Judging by all that she'd heard of the pleasant temperament of the children's regular nanny, Melissa didn't think Mrs. Butters would mind.

Lily observed Melissa's improved state with a smug and satisfied expression on her face, shrugged off her thank-yous and sped away in her minivan full of children. Melissa admired the woman's endless supply of energy and wondered if it ever ran out.

Charles appeared at two o'clock, ready to relieve Melissa of the children so she could take a nap, but she was adamant that she didn't need one. Charles wasn't going to back down at first, but Melissa convinced him that she really couldn't sleep even if she tried. After all, she'd been up less than five hours, and she'd had a leisurely morning. Finally capitulating, Charles returned to his study.

Over dinner, which Melissa made sure was especially delicious, Charles teased and talked with the children, then afterward carted them away for baths and bedtime stories while Melissa cleaned things up. She hadn't been lying to Charles that afternoon about not being tired. In fact, she felt more energetic than she had in weeks.

It was weird, going abruptly from so-tired-she-could-die to so-full-of-energy-she-might-pop. She wondered if it was that ''nesting'' instinct she'd always heard about. Even her mother had told her that just prior to giving birth she'd had the urge to clean cupboards and closets, scrub floors, cook and freeze food and generally make the house pristine-perfect in anticipation of leaving soon for the hospital and bringing home a spanking-new baby in a few days.

But Melissa had a week and a half left before her due date. Wouldn't it be a little too soon for the nesting instinct to set in? Maybe it was just the exhilaration of being around such a fun bunch of kids and their father.

Yes, their father definitely made her feel exhilarated.... Over the course of the day, she'd frequently found herself reliving those moments in his bedroom.

The way he'd looked at her when he'd seen her in his robe. First there was surprise, yes, but then there was something more.

Melissa was sure she'd seen sexual desire in Charles's expression, felt sexual tension in the air. And it wasn't just on her side, either, although her own attraction to Charles had already been fanned pretty hot during a half hour of fantasizing in the tub even before he showed up in the flesh. She hoped he hadn't noticed how her breasts had actually hardened when she saw him in the bedroom, munching on that apple!

Then, when he'd stood so close and cupped her chin in his free hand, she'd thought she'd melt on the spot. She could smell the fresh apple on his breath and wondered how it would taste if he kissed her...

Melissa wiped off the kitchen counters and looked around with a critical eye. In addition to cleaning up after dinner, she'd whipped up a cake for tomorrow's dessert. Now the cake was cooling and every kitchen utensil, dish, pot and pan she'd used was put away and every surface was spotless, but she was still looking around for something else to do. She had all this unexpected energy and didn't want to waste it. It had been weeks since she'd felt so good!

Besides, if she was finished in the kitchen, it was time to go home, and she wasn't all that keen on the idea of getting in her little hot car and driving across town to her little hot apartment.

But that was exactly what she needed to do, of course. She was enjoying playing house with Charles and his children a bit too much. It was like a perfect little pretend world away from her own reality. Her own reality, her own life, certainly wasn't bad—especially since she'd gotten rid of Brad—but it was definitely lonelier.

As Melissa hung up the dishcloth, she reminded herself that the harmony and perfection she enjoyed in this wonderful house with this wonderful family was very fragile. Once she finally picked the time and got the courage to reveal to Charles her lie about Brad, things would probably never be the same. Charles would be forced to see her for the terribly flawed person she was.

She'd called her mother that afternoon, just to check in after being gone from her apartment overnight. Melissa was surprised to hear that her mother already knew where she'd spent the night. Charles had contacted Pam the evening before, anticipating and curtailing any worry ahead of time. Melissa decided that Charles was the most considerate man she'd ever met.

Then her mother had inquired if she'd told Charles yet that she was a divorcee, not a widow. Melissa had to confess that, no, she hadn't, and her mother sighed heavily into the phone, which was marginally better than getting a long lecture from her. But the guilt effect was about the same.

"All done?"

Melissa turned to find Charles standing at the door of the kitchen, his sleeves rolled up to above his elbows, the knees of his jeans wet, looking much as he had that first morning.

"Yes," Melissa answered, shying away from making prolonged eye contact with him. As long as the children were around, she was able to act more or less naturally around Charles. But finding herself alone with him again, she felt shy and nervous.

"Hey, you even made a cake! Smells like chocolate."

"It is."

"Great. My favorite."

Melissa grabbed the dishcloth and started shining the counters again. "Well…good. Are the children already asleep?"

"Daniel went out like a light as soon as he hit the sheets. Sarah and Christopher were nodding off by the end of the third book I read to them. Lily really tired them out today with all the exercise they got at the park, and then swimming at the pool. These long days of sunshine sometimes keep them up, but tonight their usual eight o'clock bedtime worked out just right."

"I'm surprised I'm not ready for an eight o'clock bedtime, too," Melissa admitted with a chuckle. "But maybe I'll get some stuff done at home that's been begging for my attention."

She rehung the dishcloth and took tentative steps toward the door, hoping Charles would move when it was time for her to pass through. She remembered how their bodies had brushed against each other that morning and her heart skipped a beat.

Charles propped his shoulder against the doorjamb, crossed his arms and ankles and effectively barred Melissa's escape from the kitchen. Melissa stopped in her tracks, snatched a quick glance at him, then looked down at the buttons on her smock.

What now?

"You really are feeling better this evening, aren't

you?'' he said. ''Not as tired as you usually are. And you didn't even take a nap this afternoon.''

She looked up, saw the warmth and satisfaction in his eyes and quickly looked down again. ''Yes, I am. I'm not sure why, although perhaps a good night's sleep last night and the princess treatment I got this morning might account for it.''

Charles chuckled. ''Well, although it wasn't my intention, the so-called princess treatment you got this morning certainly paid off for me and the kids. That dinner was delicious, Melissa.''

''Daniel didn't think so,'' Melissa reminded him, finally daring to maintain eye contact, now that they were back to discussing the children and her job duties.

''But he liked that toddler food you gave him. Maybe you should tell me the brand and I'll have Mrs. Butters pick up a few jars when she gets back. Finding something that Daniel likes when he won't eat what the family's eating would save scraping a lot of food off the walls.''

Melissa was proud of her made-especially-for-toddlers food and was delighted that Daniel liked it so much. Her guinea pig experiment had worked out well. Despite this, she found herself a little hesitant about discussing her fledgling business with Charles…or with anyone besides her family and the stores she sold to, for that matter. But since word of mouth was a wonderful and inexpensive way to advertise, she needed to get over being so modest.

''It's called Missy's Kid Cuisine,'' Melissa finally admitted with a shy smile.

Charles's eyebrows raised. ''*Missy's* Kid Cuisine, as in Missy Richardson?''

Melissa nodded. "Yep."

Charles's eyes beamed with interest and approval. "Wow, Melissa, that's great! So you're an entrepreneur now...just like you said you'd be in high school."

She chuckled. "Yeah, only I was going to be a millionaire by now, remember?"

Charles shrugged, grinned. "So? There's still plenty of time to make your million. Besides, you've probably learned by now that making the money is great, but the actual development of the business, watching it grow, selling your product, coming up with new ideas and making them work is the real thrill of it all."

"Well, yeah, so far it's been exciting, and that's good because the money part hasn't materialized yet. Things are going well, but I just haven't been doing it very long. Just since Brad—"

Uh-oh. She'd almost let the cat out of the bag again. But Charles let it pass. After all, she'd asked him not to mention Brad or speak of his untimely demise, and he was obviously a man of his word. Of course, this would probably be a good time to spill the truth, but she couldn't bear the thought of Charles's good opinion of her changing. She just needed to keep the secret two more days!

At the last minute on the last day of her employment as the Avery children's nanny, she'd tell him that Brad was very much alive and probably lounging on a California beach with a blonde at that very moment. If Charles reacted negatively, if he didn't understand and couldn't forgive her, at least she wouldn't have to see him again.

CHARLES HAD TO bite his tongue to keep himself from asking Melissa why she hadn't started her business while Brad was still alive. Had she been too busy doing his classwork? Working extra hours to support him while he attended school? Or was Brad just not supportive of her aspirations...only his? Damn it, it was so frustrating not knowing the particulars of Melissa's marriage with Brad. Even some general knowledge of what their life had been like together would help Charles know how to proceed.

Charles stopped a second to contemplate his use of the word *proceed* in that previous thought. It meant, he supposed, that he was hoping to explore the possibility of a relationship with Melissa that went beyond that of employer/employee and former attendees of the same high school.

But he'd never know what to do, or when to do it, until he found out whether he was dealing with a good ghost or a bad ghost from Melissa's previous fourteen-year-long relationship with Brad. Was she carrying a torch, or a grudge? Or neither?

How the hell was he supposed to *proceed?*

Right now he supposed the smartest thing to do would be to speak. An awkward pause had developed since Melissa's most recent unfinished sentence containing the name of her departed husband.

"If Daniel's reaction is any proof of the tastiness of your product, Melissa," Charles said, picking up the conversation at least close to where they'd left off, "you're going to have a big success on your hands. So, tell me more. Where do you cook and process the food? Do you have many employees yet? And when do you find the time to do everything you do?"

Charles started walking out of the kitchen and into the living room. As was his intention, Melissa followed him. When he sat down, she sat down, which was also his plan. He was truly interested in her business venture, but equally interested in getting her to hang around for any reason he could think of, and for as long as possible.

With an attentive audience, Melissa became quite animated about Missy's Kid Cuisine.

"I don't really make *baby* food...you know, the pureed stuff they eat first? I specialize in toddler food, meals made especially for the stage in between carrot pulp and casseroles. As you've probably noticed, two-year-olds can be very fussy eaters. The trick is to make the food tasty and attractive to the eye—you've got to admit strained peas are *not* attractive—and then make sure it contains all the nutrition they need during that very active growth period between two to five years old."

"You've really done your homework, haven't you?" Charles said with an admiring smile. "Tell me, Melissa, is the food you use organically grown? Annette used to worry about the chemicals used in farming, not to mention the additives for extended shelf life."

"Annette was a smart mother and an informed shopper," Melissa said, sitting forward in her seat as she warmed to the subject. "Just the type of individual I created my product for. I use only organic vegetables. And as for meat..."

The conversation continued for several satisfying minutes, but eventually all the questions had been asked and answered, and Melissa stood to go.

But Charles didn't want her to go. He also rose

from his seat and asked impetuously, "Why don't you stay and watch the meteor shower with me?"

Melissa seemed startled at first by his invitation, then shy and indecisive. He was beginning to think he'd gone too far too fast, when she said, "I didn't even know there was going to be a meteor shower tonight...until I heard you talking with those girls."

Charles hadn't meant to remind Melissa of an episode that had clearly embarrassed her. Although, despite Lily's take on the situation, he still wasn't sure why. Melissa was twice as pretty as either of those students.

"Yes, well, it won't be easily observed by the naked eye in this part of the country. But with a good telescope, it will be something to see, all right. But then, I'm an astronomer, and anything going on in the sky fascinates me."

Melissa bit her inside lip and nodded. Charles thought she looked tempted to say yes, but then maybe she was just trying to come up with a tactful and polite way to say no.

"What time does it start?"

Charles looked at his watch. "In about thirty minutes I'm planning to get the telescope set up with the right coordinates. In another hour after that, the meteors will be putting on their show."

"Will...will there be others coming over?"

"I didn't invite anyone else."

"You might not have invited anyone, but I suppose people could...you know...just show up?"

That's when Charles realized that Melissa was dreading the possibility that Kimberly and Tiffany might drop by again. "Unless we've made a specific appointment to meet at the college, my students know I'm definitely off-limits in the evening,'' he told her. Smiling, he added, "It'll just be me, you and the stars, Melissa.''

Oops.

Instead of reassuring her, Charles just might have managed to scare her off completely. Her eyes had suddenly widened to the size of half-dollars.

Just me, you, and the stars, Melissa... Although he hadn't meant it to, the teasing remark had the smarmy sound of a pickup line an astronomy professor might use on a regular basis! No wonder Melissa was looking so surprised and—

"Charles, I think I need to sit down." Melissa rested one hand on her stomach and the other hand gripped the back of a nearby chair.

Charles was instantly at her side, helping her to a seat. "What's wrong? Is it the baby?"

"I'm having a contraction. At least I think that's what's happening. My stomach just tightened up like a giant fist and...and it hurt like the dickens for a minute or two.''

Charles got down on one knee in front of her. "Do you want me to call your mother?"

"No, not yet. No reason to sound the alarm yet. I'm not due for several more days, and this might be the only contraction I have tonight.''

Charles knew she was right. Annette had had false alarms with all three of her pregnancies. And it was useless to go to the hospital too soon. They just sent you home and it was such a letdown to leave without a baby.

"You're being very sensible and patient and brave," Charles remarked with a smile. "Especially since this is your first child.''

"Remember, I've only had one contraction," she emphasized, smiling. "We'll see how sensible and patient and brave I am when they're coming one after the other."

"Have you taken birthing classes?"

"Yes."

"Is your mother your coach?"

"Yes. And she'll be great at it. But I don't want to tell her about this contraction because, even though it means nothing, she'll start hovering over me till the baby comes."

Charles patted her knee. "Well, we'll see whether or not it means nothing. We'll see if there's more. If there are, I can time them for you, and if you're truly in labor, we'll call your mother."

Melissa's brows furrowed. "What about the meteor shower?"

"It's not that important," Charles said dismissively. "I've seen hundreds of them."

"Well, maybe you have, but *I* haven't," Melissa exclaimed with a laugh. "If I'm not in full-blown labor, Professor Avery, I still want to see the meteor shower. As long as it's not you, me, the stars, and a baby, I'm holding you to your invitation."

Charles laughed along with her, completely delighted and beguiled. So, she hadn't thought his pickup line was smarmy, after all. That was good news.

And the night was still young…

MELISSA WASN'T SURE what she was doing. She really had no business accepting Charles's invitation to watch the meteor shower with him. But she was enjoying his company so much and was feeling so good, the alternative of going back to her empty apartment just didn't stand a chance.

As for the contraction, Melissa wasn't terribly concerned. She knew about Braxton-Hicks, or "practice" contractions, and with a week and a half to go till her due date, she figured that's what was going on. But even if she *were* going into actual labor, the baby was far enough along to be just fine.

She hoped she wasn't in labor, though. Yesterday she might have hoped the contraction meant the baby was coming early, but she'd felt so well today, had had so much energy, she didn't mind carrying the baby a few more days. Especially since she really didn't want her nanny job to end sooner than Saturday, which was when Mrs. Butters would be back at her post. Melissa was having so much fun with the children—and, yes, with their father—she just didn't want it to end!

When no more contractions came in the space of thirty minutes, Charles checked on the children, then led Melissa through his bedroom—which brought a blush to her cheeks—and drew back burgundy drapes that covered French doors. They walked through the French doors and onto a large glassed-in deck that faced southwest.

"It's a solarium!" Melissa said, looking around appreciatively at the arrangement of comfy, casual furniture and a profusion of plants. Taking center stage, though, was a large, impressive telescope. Melissa stared at the shiny black instrument in awe—it had a definite masculine aura about it, but maybe that's because it belonged to Charles, was part of Charles—but she was soon diverted by the view.

Since Charles's house was located relatively high

in the foothills, or on the "bench," as it was locally referred to, all of Salt Lake Valley could be seen through the glass walls of the solarium. To the west, a molten red sun was sinking into the shimmering waters of the Great Salt Lake, the dusky-purple outline of Antelope Island in the background. To the east, foothills bathed in a mauve glow gave way to the scrub- and pine-covered Wasatch Mountains.

"Oh, Charles, this view is incredible. If this were my home, I'd probably spend every evening right here, watching the sun go down and the stars come out."

Charles had been standing nearby as she'd looked and admired, his hands in his pockets, a smile on his face. Now he took her by the hand and led her to a corner of the solarium and pointed toward the sky. "Well, there's the first star. Can you see it, barely twinkling through the dusk? Why don't you make a wish?"

"I thought the rule was you only made wishes on falling stars," Melissa demurred. Charles was standing so close, and he was still holding her hand. She felt warm and happy and excited.

Charles squeezed her hand and leaned close to her ear. "Let's make a new rule, just for you, Melissa. Just for tonight. Just close your eyes and make a wish."

Melissa swallowed hard. Charles's breath against her cheek was making her skin tingle and her breathing quick and shallow. She felt the baby kick and wondered if everything she was feeling, all the wondrous, joyful sensations she'd all but forgotten were possible, were being felt by her baby, too.

Melissa hoped so. She'd often wondered and worried that her divorce and all the turmoil that went with it had been hard on her pregnancy, bad for the baby. But if the baby was sharing her feelings now, nothing but good could come from it.

She closed her eyes. She made her wish.

And her water broke.

Chapter Six

Melissa was soaked, and there was still a puddle of water at her feet. Apparently her baby had been swimming around in an Olympic-size pool of amniotic fluid! Even Charles's shoes had not been spared a sprinkling.

"This is not what I wished for," she murmured, staring down at the irrefutable evidence that she was about to become a mommy, and very soon.

"It's time to call your mother, Melissa," Charles said with admirable calm as he also peered down at the puddle of water.

"But I only had the one contraction!"

"Your water broke. Believe me, contractions are next. And soon." Charles took her by the shoulders and turned her to face him. He smiled reassuringly. "Your baby's coming, Melissa. Aren't you excited?"

Melissa hesitated. She wasn't sure what she was feeling. Of course she was excited. And scared. But there was also this silly, selfish side of her that wished the baby had waited to be born till she could have finished out her week in the Avery household.

Once she was no longer needed as their nanny, she might never see the children—or their father—again.

She'd miss them so much…

Charles bent to peer into her eyes, which she very much feared were full of unshed tears. "Melissa, what's wrong? Are you having a contraction?"

Melissa was about to say no truthfully, but she was suddenly in the middle of a much stronger contraction than the one she'd had thirty minutes earlier.

"Oh! Oh, yeah, I'm definitely having a contraction," she admitted, resting her hands on her stomach. "It hurts, and…and my stomach feels as hard as a rock."

Charles put an arm around her shoulder and looked at his watch. "Tell me when it's over."

Seconds ticked by. Melissa was surprised by the length of the contraction and the severity of the pain. She squeezed her eyes shut and took deep breaths.

When the contraction was finally over, she found herself leaning into Charles for support.

"Pretty strong?" he asked gently.

"Well, I've never had a baby before so I can't compare, but, yeah, it sure felt strong to me."

Charles led her inside and helped her sit on the edge of the bed. "Do you want to lie down?"

Melissa shook her head. "No."

Charles picked up the phone by his bed. "Tell me your mom's number."

Melissa told him the number and he punched it in. After several seconds, it was obvious that no one was answering.

"Doesn't she have an answering machine?" Charles asked.

"Yes, but maybe Dad's on the Internet."

"What about a second number or a cell phone?"

Melissa gave him her mother's cell phone number. He dialed, waited, then left a message. "Mrs. Richardson, this is Charles Avery. Melissa's water broke. Call me as soon as you get this message at my home phone, or my cell phone if I'm not here. My numbers are…"

He gave her the numbers, then turned and looked with concern at Melissa.

"Why did you give her your cell phone number? Where are you going, Charles?" Melissa joked.

"Probably to the hospital," he told her matter-of-factly.

She laughed. "It will be hours before—"

But she didn't finish her sentence. She was seized with another contraction, this one harder than the last. Charles gave her his hand to grip and looked at his watch.

By the time the pain was gone, Melissa had beads of perspiration on her upper lip.

"Your contractions are only three minutes apart, Melissa. And they're lasting longer. I'm going to have to take you to the hospital."

"But I've only had three contractions, Charles! Just *three!*"

"Sometimes that's the way it happens. You may be one of those lucky ladies who have quick labors."

"Not if the baby comes before I can get to the hospital!"

"Precisely. That's why we're not going to wait till your mother calls back."

"But what about the children?"

Charles had already picked up the phone again.

"I'm calling Lily. If she isn't home, we'll wake up the children and take them with us."

Melissa couldn't believe this! One minute she was enjoying a fantastic view with a fantastic man, and the next minute she was soaking wet and cramped with pain every three—no, make that every *two*—minutes. She was already having another contraction. Charles looked at her with sympathetic concern as he waited for his sister to answer the phone. She closed her eyes and did the breathing exercises she'd been taught in her birthing classes.

"Lily? Thank God you're home. Is Josh there? Good. Can he watch the kids? Good. Can you watch *my* kids? Because Melissa's in labor, that's why, and I need to get her to the hospital. Get over here as fast as you can, okay?"

Charles slammed down the phone and hurried to Melissa's side again. "She only lives a mile away. She'll be here in less than five minutes."

Melissa nodded, gritting her teeth as she waited out the contraction. When it was over, she opened her eyes and tried to smile. "Boy, you never signed up for this, did you?"

Charles smiled back and gently smoothed the hair away from her damp forehead. "I'm just glad you were with me and not all alone and unable to reach your mother."

"You should just put me in a cab," she advised him with a weak smile.

"What? And miss out on all the excitement? Listen, Missy, we'd better start for the garage while you're in between contractions. Can you stand?"

"Of course." She stood up, felt cramping, but was

perfectly able to walk as long as she didn't have another hard contraction.

He put his arm around her shoulder and they walked out of the bedroom and down the long hall to the mud room, which connected to the garage. As they opened the door to the garage, a blast of hot air hit Melissa in the face.

"Geez, how hot did it get today?"

"I don't know. It was 108 yesterday. If we have more summers like this one, I guess I'll need to get temperature control for the garage," Charles said, still holding onto Melissa as they walked around the front of the car to the passenger side. By the time Melissa was seated in the front seat of Charles's navy-blue SUV, Melissa felt sick to her stomach. Even though Charles had left the front windows down, it was still hotter in the car than in the garage.

Then another contraction started. When it was over, she said, "You'd better check on the kids one more time."

"I checked on them just before we went into the solarium, remember? They were just fine. And I don't want to leave you, Melissa. Lily will be here in a second and she'll check on them first thing," Charles said.

"I want you to give them a kiss for me," Melissa persisted, fighting tears as she thought again about how today might be the last time she'd ever see them. She forced a smile. "Hey, don't argue with an about-to-deliver pregnant lady, okay?"

Charles looked at her worriedly. "Okay, but first I'm pulling the car out of the garage and turning on the air-conditioning."

Melissa didn't argue with this. The heat was stifling.

By the time Charles had backed the car out of the garage and came back from checking on the kids, Lily's minivan had pulled up by the driver's side. Charles pressed the button to roll down the window and said, "Thanks, Lily. You're a godsend. I'll call you." Then he immediately backed out of the driveway, giving Lily no chance to do anything other than wave, smile and do a thumb's up. Melissa tried to smile back, but she was in a lot of pain.

University Hospital was less than ten minutes away, but the trip seemed like an endless blur to Melissa. She was pretty much cramping all the time now, and she knew the contractions must be less than two minutes apart.

She bit her lip to keep from crying out, but Charles must have seen her attempt at ladylike self-control. "Don't be shy in front of me, Melissa. Moan or curse or scream, or do whatever helps."

Melissa nodded, appreciating his advice but hoping she wouldn't have to take it. Two contractions later, she was moaning. Three contractions later, she cupped her hand over her mouth to muffle a scream. On the fourth contraction she cursed under her breath.

Charles squeezed her hand. "That's my girl. Hold on. We're almost there."

The radio was on, probably because they were both too busy and preoccupied to turn it off, and Melissa heard a cheerful weather forecaster say it had reached 107 degrees that day. It was the fifth day in a row of temperatures over 105, typical for southern Utah, but unprecedented for the northern part of the

state. It was a new record, in fact. And it was still
hovering near the century mark even though it was
past nine o'clock at night.

In another couple of minutes, Charles pulled up in
front of the emergency-room entrance, ran inside and
returned almost instantly with an orderly and a
wheelchair.

Melissa was helped into the chair and wheeled into
the hospital. Charles was instructed to move the
SUV, which he did most reluctantly after giving Melissa a quick kiss on the cheek and promising, "I'll
be right back, kiddo. Hang in there."

By the time he returned, Melissa had been put in
a hospital gown, helped onto a gurney and checked
by the nurse. She was fully effaced and already up
to eight centimeters.

"We've called her doctor and he's on his way, but
he might not make it in time. There's an excellent
Ob/Gyn upstairs, though, just finishing up another
delivery. We're taking her immediately to the maternity floor," the nurse informed Charles as she and
the orderly wheeled the gurney toward the elevator.
"You'd better fill out the papers later if you want to
be around when your baby's born."

Melissa could see a fleeting startled look in
Charles's eyes, which was quickly replaced by a
thoughtful expression. Of course they'd assume
Charles was the father, and Melissa guessed he was
debating whether or not he should inform them of
their mistake. Maybe he decided it wasn't worth the
trouble, or maybe he thought he'd be of better use
to Melissa if, as the baby's father, he had all the
privileges attached to that distinction. In either case,
he said nothing to the nurse.

He did, however, ask for Melissa's approval. As they waited for some people to get off the elevator so they could get on, he bent near her ear and whispered, "Well, what's the verdict, Missy? Do you want me to stay or go?"

Melissa's eyes filled with grateful tears. "I want you to stay, Charles. If you don't mind?"

He kissed her, this time on the lips. Just briefly, but so tenderly and sweetly. Melissa had imagined a first kiss with Charles, but she'd never in a million years imagined it would be while she was lying on a gurney, her knees poking up like two sharp mountain peaks under the white sheet that covered her, dressed in a very unsexy hospital-issue gown and intermittently groaning from the pain.

Besides the nurse—a thirtyish blonde—and the young, muscular male orderly with dark hair pulled back into a short ponytail, they were followed onto the elevator by a diminutive elderly woman with white spun-sugar hair, dressed in a coral-pink volunteer jacket and black slacks. She was pushing a rolling library of paperback books. Her nametag read Hester.

As the elevator doors closed, Hester smiled benignly at Melissa. "It will be over soon, my dear, and you'll have a beautiful baby in your arms to make up for all this pain and trouble."

Since Melissa had just started another contraction, she only managed a polite grimace before beginning her breathing exercises. Charles bent near, coaching her.

Melissa's eyes were closed, but she felt the elevator's gentle lurch as it began moving. The labor and delivery rooms were on the sixth floor and they had boarded on the main level. Soon she'd be giving birth. She'd been told that she was too far along to get an epidural, which wasn't the best news she'd had that day…

"You make a lovely couple," Hester cooed. "Is this your first baby?"

Melissa opened her eyes, relieved to see that the elderly woman was addressing Charles this time and she'd be spared the trouble of responding. She was, however, curious as to what Charles would answer.

"Well…no," Charles answered distractedly.

The nurse looked at Melissa. "You did say this was *your* first baby, didn't you?"

"Yes, it's *her* first," Charles answered, a little impatiently—after all, he was trying to coach Melissa's breathing and he kept getting interrupted. "But not *my* first."

Hester nodded sagely. "Ah, I see. It's your second marriage. You don't meet many couples still in their first marriages these days, do you? Are you divorced or widowed?"

This time Charles pretended not to hear and the orderly, standing behind Hester, grinned and rolled his eyes. "Hester, you're being too nosy again. What did I tell you about that?"

Hester chuckled self-consciously. "Well, Nathan, I'm just interested in people, that's all. This is my first day as a volunteer, you see, and I guess I'm just not sure what the difference is between being nosy and just being friendly."

"If you want my opinion," the orderly offered, still with that good-natured grin, "if your question is ignored, or the person you're talking to abruptly changes the subject or comments about the weather, you're being too nosy.''

Hester nodded appreciatively, not the least bit offended by Nathan's well-meaning advice. "Ah, I see. But I'm sure the young lady won't mind my asking if she's having a boy or a girl...will she?'' She raised her wispy, white brows and smiled at Melissa.

Finally done with her contraction, Melissa was spent, exhausted, depleted. She wasn't sure how she was going to find the energy to push this baby out. Her throat was dry and she was wishing she had the crushed ice they'd left behind in the ER cubicle, but she managed to reply in a raspy voice, "No, I don't mind you asking, but I honestly don't know, Hester. I wanted to be surprised."

Hester had opened her mouth to say something else, when the elevator sort of bounced then creaked to a sudden stop. The lights flickered, then gave out, leaving them in utter darkness.

"Oh, good gracious," Hester squeaked. "What's happening?"

The orderly muttered, "Perfect. Just perfect."

The nurse ordered, "Stay calm, everyone. The emergency generator will come on in a minute or two."

Charles bent closer to Melissa—she could feel his breath against her cheek—and whispered, "Don't worry, Melissa. I'm right here, sweetie." Then he kissed her damp forehead.

Melissa said nothing. She couldn't. She was in too much pain. She was having the hardest contraction so far, and felt an almost overwhelming urge to push. Scared and not too proud to admit it, she clutched Charles's shirt front and croaked, "I don't want to have this baby on an elevator, Charles. What if something goes wrong? What if the baby needs—''

Charles rubbed her shoulder soothingly. ''The elevator should start moving any second, Melissa.''

''But I'm going to *give birth* any second,'' Melissa wailed. ''I want to push. I *have* to push!''

''No, don't push!'' shouted the nurse.

Suddenly the lights flickered on, but they weren't as bright as before. Obviously the main power was still out and the generator was supplying the electricity.

Melissa blinked and looked around. The nurse stood waiting and listening nervously by the emergency phone, her hand hovering near the receiver, as if expecting the elevator to start moving any minute and eliminating the need for any calls for help.

''It's not moving,'' the orderly stated unnecessarily.

Hester was clinging to the orderly's arm. ''Why isn't it moving, Nathan?''

''I don't know. Maybe all the power's being diverted to surgery. We got several critical emergencies late this afternoon.''

''I think you'd better get on the phone,'' Charles tersely prompted the nurse. ''*Now.* Let someone know there's a woman stuck on this elevator, about to give birth.''

The nurse picked up the receiver. ''This has happened before,'' she muttered. ''But the elevator has always started moving shortly after the lights came on.''

''Well, there's a first time for everything,'' Nathan observed philosophically, as he patted Hester's clinging fingers. ''But no one's ever had a baby in the elevator at this hospital before. I know, I asked once.''

''I don't intend to be the first!'' Melissa exclaimed, but her next contraction and the urge to push seemed to indicate otherwise.

The nurse talked briefly on the phone, explaining their situation in a low voice. When she got off she said, ''Nathan was right. The power's being diverted to surgery and I.C.U. There are some complicated surgeries in progress and they're right at the crucial stages. Lots of respirators and a couple of by-pass machines are being used.''

Charles couldn't believe what was happening! He knew that most births were without complications, but if there were complications, being on an elevator with no access to even the most basic medical supplies was a decided disadvantage. In fact, it was downright dangerous.

''I would certainly call this a crucial situation, too,'' Charles responded to the nurse, his words pointed, but spoken in a quiet tone so as not to alarm Melissa any more than she was already. ''Did you tell them that?''

''I told them I had a woman about to deliver, and they said they should be able to get power to the elevators in just a few minutes.'' Charles was relieved when she seemed to ''buck up'' at this point and realize what needed to be done. She smiled reassuringly at Melissa. ''I'm not an OB nurse, so I don't normally help deliver babies, but we've had a few that couldn't wait till we got their moms upstairs that were born in the Emergency Room, and I've assisted once or twice.''

By now the nurse was at Melissa's side, holding

her other hand, exuding the kind of calm confidence needed in this situation. "We can pull this off, Melissa, if we need to. If the baby's born in this elevator, it won't be long before we're rescued and everything will be done to make sure you and your baby are perfectly healthy and no worse for the experience."

The nurse's composed demeanor and warm manner were helping to reassure Melissa. Charles was feeling better, too, and gave a silent prayer of thanks. He was beginning to think he was going to have to deliver Melissa's baby all on his own, with the available hospital staff as mere onlookers.

"My name is Lana, by the way," the nurse continued.

"Pleased…to…meet you, Lana," Melissa said with a groan. "But if you don't mind, I've got to push!"

Lana turned to Nathan and Hester. "You two move over there, give Melissa some privacy."

Nathan and Hester shuffled over a few feet, which was as far as they could go in the close confines of the elevator. Privacy was really not a realistic goal in the circumstances, but Melissa would probably later appreciate the attempt. Right now all she wanted to do was push…which, from Charles's experience watching the births of his own three children, meant the baby was coming, ready or not.

Lana pushed up the sheet and nudged Melissa's knees apart. Charles watched Lana's face as she checked Melissa. The furrow between her brow told all.

"He or she is about to crown, Melissa."

"Yes, I know," Melissa said faintly. "I can feel it. I *told* you I needed to push."

"Well, hon, I'm not going to ask you to hold back any longer. Go ahead and push."

There had been no time to put a heart monitor on the baby in the Emergency Room, and no one had expected them to get stuck in the elevator. But without the monitor, how the baby was doing as it made its way down the final stretch of the birth canal was anyone's guess. If the baby was in any kind of distress, the sooner he or she was born, the better. Charles knew this, the nurse knew this, and Melissa probably did, too.

So…Melissa was going to make history. Her baby was going to be the first baby born in the Salt Lake City University Hospital elevator! Charles just hoped the story that would be repeated over the years would have a happy ending, with both mother and baby coming out of this experience healthy and nontraumatized.

Charles supported Melissa's back as she leaned into the next contraction, pushing with all her might. Her eyes were squeezed shut, her brow furrowed, her teeth gritted with the effort of giving birth…but to Charles she looked beautiful. He was in awe of her courage and endurance in the face of such pain, uncertainty and inconvenience. Never in a million years would he have thought, as a teenager, that he'd be by Missy Richardson's side, holding her hand, cheering her on, as she brought into the world her first child!

If only it were his child…

"One or two more pushes ought to do it, Melissa," the nurse said. "The baby's position looks good. On the next contraction, give it all you've got, okay, hon?''

Melissa nodded, looking thoroughly spent, the perspiration dripping down her forehead. Charles took the edge of the sheet that was covering her and wiped her face. She smiled up at him weakly, the corners of her mouth twitching from the effort. "Thank you for being here, Charles. I don't think I could have done it without—"

The next contraction seized her and Melissa grimaced, then bore down, her face turning red with the effort.

"Here it comes!" the nurse exclaimed with satisfaction. "The head's out. Oh, look at all that black hair!"

"Why isn't it crying?" Melissa demanded breathlessly.

"He or she's not all the way out yet, Melissa," the nurse answered. "I'm clearing its mouth. Push one more time, hon. Just once more."

Melissa didn't look like she had the energy left for one more push, but she took a deep breath and bore down again.

"It's a boy!" the nurse nearly shouted. "A big boy, too. I'd say at least eight pounds."

Melissa tried to see around her own up-drawn knees. "He's still not crying. Is he okay?"

The nurse appeared to be using the sheets to clean the baby up and was probably looking him over to make sure he had the usual ten fingers and toes. "He's got good color, Melissa. Doesn't look like he was in any kind of distress."

"Thank God." Melissa's voice was choked with

emotion. "But please, Lana, please let me hold my baby."

Finally the nurse held the baby up where everyone could see him, and right on cue he crinkled up his little red face and squalled.

Charles felt an overwhelming surge of emotion. Tears stung his eyes. Normally he never cried, but witnessing birth always did something to him on a visceral level. He'd always thought it was because he'd been witnessing the birth of his own children. This little boy wasn't his, but he already felt a connection.

Hester gasped and said, "Oh my. Oh my heavens," over and over again.

Nathan grunted a manly, "Way to go, Melissa. He looks like a future quarterback."

Nathan's comment brought home again to Charles the fact that the baby's father was Brad Baxter, who had, indeed, been a quarterback in high school and college.

This baby is Brad's son, Charles lectured himself. *Not yours. As much as you wish it was different, you might as well face facts.*

"Good work, Mom," he whispered in Melissa's ear, setting aside his own silly and hopeless desires. "You have a beautiful baby boy."

Melissa held out her arms and the nurse said, "He's still attached by the umbilical cord. The best I can do is lay him on your stomach."

Charles could see Melissa was disappointed. He pulled out his Swiss Army knife and offered it to the nurse. "Would it be too unsanitary to use this?"

"I've got anibacterial wipes in my smock pocket," Hester piped up, eager to be helpful.

Lana hesitated for a moment, then said, "That'll work, but first we need to tie off the cord." She looked down and scanned everyone's shoes. "Give me one of your shoelaces, Nathan. I'm sure this proud papa will buy you a new pair."

Nathan quickly got down on one knee and removed the long lace from one of his athletic shoes. Lana took the lace and the knife, quickly rubbed them down with Hester's antibacterial wipes, then tied off the cord and cut it. She handed the baby to Melissa and a hushed reverence filled the elevator. Hushed except for the joyous sound of a crying baby.

As Melissa looked down into the face of her newborn, she instantly forgave him for the pain connected with bringing him into the world and for every naughty thing he might do during his entire childhood. Love swelled in her chest till it hurt. She felt warm tears trickle down her cheek and off her chin. One teardrop plopped on the baby's nose and he squalled even louder.

Melissa laughed. "No problem with his lungs."

"No apparent problem with anything," the nurse commented. "But as soon as this elevator gets going, we'll check him over thoroughly. And you, too, Melissa. You're not quite done yet, you know. You haven't expelled the placenta."

Melissa was just glad her baby was finally there, safe and sound. She was dizzy with happiness.

No, wait… She was dizzy with more than happiness. Heck, she was just plain dizzy… Her head felt light, like a balloon. She looked at the nurse and said, "Suddenly I don't feel very well."

The nurse looked down at the sheet and saw what

everyone else saw at the same moment, including Melissa. Her legs were flat on the gurney now, but there was a pool of red spreading out from underneath her. She could feel the sticky warmth of her own blood, but somehow couldn't comprehend that it was coming from her.

The nurse's eyes widened and she hurried over to the emergency phone. "We need you to get this elevator moving right now!" she shouted urgently into the phone. "I've got a newborn in here and a mother who might be bleeding out from a tear in the uterus wall!"

Melissa thought the nurse's voice seemed far away and fuzzy. And suddenly she didn't have the strength to hold her baby. She felt her arms slacken and she was afraid she was going to drop her precious child. But Charles gently lifted the baby out of her arms.

She looked up to thank him, but she couldn't seem to get the words out. She tried to smile into Charles's beautiful green eyes, but she must not have been managing that very well, either, because Charles's eyes were full of worry and alarm.

It would probably be best if she just closed her eyes and rested.

Yes. That was better...

Chapter Seven

The next five minutes were hell on earth for Charles. When the hospital powers-that-be understood that the situation on the elevator was life-or-death, they immediately ordered that energy be diverted to the elevator to get it moving again.

Meanwhile, Melissa was unconscious and looked pale as a ghost. Charles held her baby against his chest, trying to keep him warm. The volunteer, with great presence of mind, took off her smock and handed it to Charles to wrap the baby in it. "That should help," Hester whispered worriedly.

But there wasn't a damn thing any of them could do to help Melissa! Charles wanted to shout. The nurse was packing her with sheets to try to stop the flow of blood, but they all knew she needed medical attention and she needed it right away!

Charles thanked God and all the divine powers of the universe when the elevator lurched into motion again and they traveled to the sixth floor. He stared at Melissa, willing her to revive, to somehow miraculously heal herself, to live.

To live.

Charles couldn't bear the thought of her dying.

The helplessness he felt now was too much like those hours he'd waited while Annette was in surgery, the doctors feverishly trying to repair all the damage done from the car accident. It had all seemed so unfair. She was too young. She was a mother. She was the woman he loved.

Just like Melissa.

As the elevator door opened, hospital staff converged on them. The baby was taken from Charles and whisked away down the hall, along with Melissa. Charles tried to follow, but a clerk of some kind detained him, explaining, ''I'm sorry, sir. You'll have to wait out here.''

Charles nodded numbly, his eyes fixed on the double doors through which Melissa and the baby had disappeared.

''Why don't you go downstairs and fill out the admissions forms?'' the clerk gently suggested. ''It needs to be done, and it would be a good way to pass the time while you wait.''

Charles turned to the clerk. ''But I don't have the information needed for those forms.''

The clerk, a twentysomething woman with frizzy, honey-blond hair and a sweet face, looked puzzled. ''What do you mean? Aren't you the husband?''

Charles shook his head sadly. ''No, I'm not. There is no husband. The baby's father is deceased. Melissa's mother should be here soon, though, and I'm sure she could—''

''Charles? Yes, that's him, George. Charles!''

Charles looked up and was relieved to see Melissa's mother hurrying toward him, looking not much different than she'd looked thirteen years ago. He assumed the tall, lanky man at Pam's side was

Melissa's father. They'd both just come from the direction of the stairwell door and were a little winded, obviously from climbing the six floors to get there.

"You got my message," Charles said, wondering how much they knew. By their cheerful demeanor, he figured they didn't know everything they should.

"Yes. I called the house first and your sister Lily told us you'd taken Melissa to the hospital. I tried your cell phone on the way over here, but all the lines were tied up. There's a city-wide blackout, you know! A power overload from all the air conditioners going at full-tilt, I guess."

"All the traffic lights are down and we had a hell of a time getting here," George further explained. He mopped his damp brow.

"They told us you guys got stuck in the elevator, so we climbed the stairs to this floor, figuring you'd show up eventually," Pam continued, then smiled brightly. "So, how far along is Missy's labor?" Without waiting for Charles's answer, she turned to her husband and added excitedly, "My labors were always pretty short, remember, George? So we'd probably better get in there right away if we want to see our grandchild born."

"The baby was born on the elevator," Charles quickly told them, preventing them from hurrying away and finding out from someone else.

They both looked stunned. "Is...is the baby all right?" Pam asked.

"Yes, he's fine," Charles said.

"A boy," George repeated, grinning. "I knew it was going to be a boy."

Finally picking up on Charles's sober mood, Pam's face suddenly clouded. "But something's wrong, isn't it, Charles? Melissa's all right, too, isn't she?"

"Pam, Melissa was bleeding a lot when we got off the elevator. She…she fainted. They just took her back, so that's all I know. I think you'd better let someone know who you are."

Charles remembered the clerk he'd been talking to, but turned around and saw she'd gone back to her desk and was on the phone. "Since you're related, I'm sure they'll let you know what's going on."

Pam's complexion had turned deathly pale. She clamped her hand over her mouth and stood as still as a statue.

"Don't immediately expect the worst, Pam," her husband advised her, although he'd grown pretty pale himself. He took her gently by the elbow. "Come on, let's see what we can find out from the clerk."

They started to walk away, but Pam turned back and said to Charles, "Thank you for being with her, Charles. Thank you for getting her here."

Charles nodded miserably. "Do you mind if I hang around in the waiting room? I won't feel like going home until I know for sure she's all right."

Pam nodded, tried to smile, then she and George walked to the clerk's desk, Pam leaning into her husband for support. Charles sighed and looked around for a sign indicating where the waiting room was.

He saw the sign, went to the room, sat in a chair, held his head in his hands and…waited.

MELISSA WOKE UP in a softly-lit hospital room. It took her a moment to get her bearings, then it all came back to her in a rush. Her water breaking, the trip to the hospital, the elevator, the pain, the birth…

The baby. *Her* baby. And Charles with her, coaching her through it, reassuring her the whole time.

Then she remembered blacking out... What had caused that, for heaven's sake? And what about her baby? Was he all right?

She sat up quickly, bringing on a little dizzy spell and some pain in too many places to count. She lay back down, closed her eyes for a second, regained her equilibrium, then looked around the room. If she couldn't find a nurse, she'd press the call button and get her in there. She wanted to know where her baby—

That's when she saw him. In a clear plastic crib close to her bed, her baby was wrapped up in a blue blanket, sleeping peacefully. Melissa's anxiety relieved, she sighed contentedly and then made a more thorough examination of her surroundings.

University Hospital was up on the east bench with a view overlooking the city, just like at Charles's house. She saw city lights twinkling outside her hospital window, so she assumed the blackout was over, or at least over downtown. In closer quarters, she observed that she was the only patient in the room. She was hooked up to an IV and a heart monitor, and had an oxygen catheter in her nose. She understood the IV part, but why the heart monitor and the oxygen catheter?

A nurse strode in just in time to answer Melissa's questions. She was tall, black and bosomy and quite gorgeous. She smiled broadly at Melissa.

"So, you're awake! Good. That baby of yours is going to be waking up pretty soon, too, and wanting more than the sugar water we gave him an hour ago. Are you breast feeding?"

"Yes, I'd planned to, but how long—"

"Good, always better for the baby in the beginning. Are you hungry?" The nurse bustled around the bed, checking the blinking and beeping monitors and various equipment.

"No, not really. How long have I—"

"You need to eat. You're still eating for two, you know."

"Of course. But how long have I been asleep? And why did I black out? I think I was bleeding—"

"Honey, you were bleeding, all right. We had to give you two liters of blood." She stopped bustling for a moment and took out Melissa's oxygen catheter. "You don't need this anymore. And by the way—" She pointed to her nametag. "My name is Lorena, but everyone calls me Rena for short."

"Why was I bleeding, Rena?"

"The placenta didn't detach from the uterine wall like it should," she explained, fluffing up an extra pillow from the foot of the bed and carefully placing it behind Melissa so she could sit up a little. "The tearing caused some bleeding. The doctors repaired the tear—"

"I had surgery?" Melissa winced as she settled her sore body into a sitting position.

"No, they did it without an incision, and if you want more details than that, Mrs. Baxter, you'll have to ask the doctors. The good news is that as soon as you got some blood, your blood pressure and heart rhythm returned to normal. And to answer your first question, you've been asleep for three hours. It's one o'clock in the morning."

Melissa looked toward the door. "So, does that mean that anyone who might have come to see me—

or been here from the beginning—has gone home for the night?"

Rena straightened Melissa's bed and folded the top sheet just under her arms. "If you're talking about your mother and dad, they're still camped out in the waiting room."

Melissa nodded. "Good. Er…is there anyone else?"

The nurse stopped the tucking-in process and smiled coyly. "Could you be referring to that good-lookin' redhead I saw in there? The one who was with you when you came to the hospital? The one who held your hand in the elevator?"

Melissa felt herself blushing. Too bad she still had more than enough blood for *that.* "Yes."

"He was in there five minutes ago, last time I looked."

Melissa felt a flood of happiness. It was silly, of course. Charles was probably just worried about her and was too responsible to leave till he knew for sure she was okay.

"So, I guess my parents told you the whole story? About the elevator and all."

"Honey, the whole hospital knows the whole story! Word got around pretty fast. Then, that new volunteer, Hester, called Channel Five News."

Melissa was incredulous. "What? *Why?*"

"I guess she thought you were a pretty good human interest story. You know…something warm and fuzzy for those feel-good three minutes they tag on to the end of twenty-seven minutes of war, crime, the economy and the weather. Of course, she didn't call until everyone knew you were going to be okay."

"Well, that's nice, I guess," Melissa said, feeling more embarrassed than anything. "I don't suppose Channel Five thought I was newsworthy enough, though."

"That's where you're wrong, Mrs. Baxter. Not only is there a reporter from Channel Five in the waiting room, but one from Channel Four and another one from Channel Two."

Now Melissa was beyond incredulous. "Honestly? But what are they waiting for, exactly? Surely they don't think I'm going to give them an interview tonight?"

Rena shook her head firmly. "No, I know they don't think that. Your mother and father set them straight on that right away. They told them that whether or not you were interviewed was up to you, and that they weren't going to get any facts out of them, either, until you'd given your permission."

"My parents are pretty protective."

Rena rested her fists on her generous hips. "Listen, honey, if you want me to, I can send those reporters packin' and tell them not to come back at all. Or I can tell them to call tomorrow. You'll know by then whether or not you want to give them an interview."

Melissa certainly understood the reporters hanging around, trying to get a story. And she was actually kind of flattered by the attention. But most of all, she was thinking that it might actually be an opportunity for her to get some wonderful publicity for Missy's Kid Cuisine. Feeling impetuous and unusually hopeful—maybe it was her latest hormone swing, this one a really big one—she made up her mind quickly.

Play the Romance Crossword Game

and get...
2 FREE BOOKS

and a
FREE GIFT...

YOURS to KEEP!

Scratch Here!

to reveal the hidden words.
Look below to see what you get.

Yes!

I have scratched off the gold areas. Please send me my **2 FREE BOOKS** and **FREE GIFT** for which I qualify. I understand that I am under no obligation to purchase any books as explained on the back of this card.

354 HDL DRTY	154 HDL DRUG

FIRST NAME   LAST NAME

ADDRESS

APT.#   CITY

STATE/PROV.   ZIP/POSTAL CODE

Visit us online at
www.eHarlequin.com

ROMANCE	MYSTERY	NOVEL	GIFT
You get **2 FREE BOOKS** PLUS a **FREE GIFT!**	You get **2 FREE BOOKS!**	You get **1 FREE BOOK!**	You get a **FREE MYSTERY GIFT!**

The Harlequin Reader Service® — Here's how it works:

Accepting your 2 free books and mystery gift places you under no obligation to buy anything. You may keep the books and gift and return the shipping statement marked "cancel." If you do not cancel, about a month later we'll send you 4 additional books and bill you just $3.99 each in the U.S., or $4.74 each in Canada, plus 25¢ shipping & handling per book and applicable taxes if any.* That's the complete price and — compared to cover prices of $4.75 each in the U.S. and $5.75 each in Canada — it's quite a bargain! You may cancel at any time, but if you choose to continue, every month we'll send you 4 more books, which you may either purchase at the discount price or return to us and cancel your subscription.

*Terms and prices subject to change without notice. Sales tax applicable in N.Y. Canadian residents will be charged applicable provincial taxes and GST. Credit or Debit balances in a customer's account(s) may be offset by any other outstanding balance owed by or to the customer

If offer card is missing write to: Harlequin Reader Service, 3010 Walden Ave., P.O. Box 1867, Buffalo NY 14240-1867

BUSINESS REPLY MAIL

FIRST-CLASS MAIL   PERMIT NO. 717-003   BUFFALO, NY

POSTAGE WILL BE PAID BY ADDRESSEE

HARLEQUIN READER SERVICE
3010 WALDEN AVE
PO BOX 1867
BUFFALO NY 14240-9952

NO POSTAGE
NECESSARY
IF MAILED
IN THE
UNITED STATES

''Rena, I think I'm going to take you up on your offer. If you don't mind..?''

''I said I'd do it, didn't I?''

''It would be great if you told the reporters to call me in the morning. Tell them I'll set up a time for an interview then. And tell them that it'll be in plenty of time for airing on the six o'clock news.''

Rena smiled. ''Okay, Mrs. Baxter. I'll do just that.''

''And please just call me Melissa.'' Her last name was still officially Baxter, but she was going to legally change that as soon as she had a spare minute. She'd be Ms. Richardson as soon as she could get the paperwork done.

''Okay, Melissa.''

Rena was turning to go, but Melissa stopped her again. ''Oh, and tell my parents to come see me, please. I'm not too tired for visitors. I know the hospital probably has visiting hours, but in this situation—''

Rena nodded indulgently. ''Yes, it's all right. I'm sure your parents won't be happy till they see you awake and talking your head off like this. Then they'll go home and sleep like babies.''

''Charles can come, too, can't he, if…if he's still here? And…and if he wants to?''

Rena chuckled. ''Don't worry. I'll make sure he knows he's invited, too. Anything else before I go, Melissa?''

Melissa smiled. ''Yes, one more thing. Would you please bring me my baby? I'm *aching* to hold him.''

CHARLES WAS A little reluctant about tagging along with Melissa's parents when the nurse came out to deliver her messages. He was thrilled to hear that Melissa was awake and doing very well, and he'd love to see her. But he didn't want to intrude on her family and push himself into their private moments together.

But when he tried to bow out gracefully, the nurse became adamant that Melissa wanted him to come, and Pam and George insisted he come, too.

"You can visit with her first, then we'll stay a little longer after you go," Pam said to make him feel less intrusive, he supposed. They had both been very nice as they sat together in the waiting room. They didn't talk much, though, because the reporters were hovering and he knew Pam and George didn't want to talk with them until Melissa had given her permission. The reporters had approached him, but he'd put them off till he could talk to Melissa, too.

But if Melissa wanted *his* opinion, she, at least, should give an interview to the media. It would be an ideal—and completely free—way of getting some good publicity for Missy's Kid Cuisine.

As he followed Pam and George into the hospital room, his first glimpse of Melissa was of her blond head bent over her baby. She was gazing into his face and gently touching his cheek as she held him close against her. She looked up as they entered, and there was a residual softness in her expression, evidence of the kind of dreamy wonder and adoration mothers feel for their newborn infants. He remembered that same look on Annette's face after the birth of each of their three children.

Charles held back, standing at the end of the bed, as Pam and George kissed and hugged their daughter and exclaimed over their new grandchild. He caught

Melissa's eye, though, and she smiled shyly at him. After all she'd been through, he thought she looked beautiful, radiant. He smiled back, lifting his hand in a silent greeting, feeling a little foolish and—yes— intrusive. But the awkwardness was worth it, just to be able to see her like this…sitting up, smiling, holding her baby.

Charles had had plenty of time for thinking and analyzing his feelings for Melissa while waiting to hear whether or not she was going to be okay. That first horrible, uncertain hour made him painfully aware that he didn't want to lose her. Not this way, not *any* way. But he didn't have a clue how she felt about him.

Accidental circumstances had thrown them together again after thirteen years, then put them in a dramatic situation that had the potential to create a bond between total strangers. Was the closeness they'd shared a temporary result of unusual circumstances, or could it lead to something more?

And if it could lead to something more, when would be the appropriate time to *try* for something more? He still didn't know exactly how she felt about the passing of her husband. Whatever she felt, those feelings might only be magnified by the birth of the child they'd created together.

By the time Melissa's relieved and doting parents finally made way for Charles, smiling their encouragement for him to approach the bed, he was feeling awkward again. He really had no business being there. Sure, Melissa and her parents would understand that he'd been worried and wanted to make sure she was okay, but he'd known she was going to be okay for the past two hours.

"Come here, Charles," Melissa said with a big smile. "How am I supposed to talk to you if you stand so far away? Besides, don't you want to see the baby now that he's been all cleaned up?"

Encouraged, Charles moved to stand beside her bed, close enough to talk and to see and to even touch, if he dared. He didn't dare, but Melissa did. She grabbed his hand and squeezed it, peering up at him from under her long, dark lashes to smile and say, "Charles, I just want to thank you. If not for your help and support, I don't know how I'd have got through this whole ordeal. I'm so glad you were there for me...and for my baby."

Charles was uncomfortable with all this gratitude. But he didn't want to say, "Anyone would have done what I did," although that was probably eighty-five-percent true. If he minimized what he did, it would be like minimizing his feelings. He'd helped Melissa while feeling much more than the average altruism of a stranger-turned-Good Samaritan. He cared for her...deeply.

"I'm just glad you're okay," he finally managed, his words hardly skimming the surface of what he truly felt. "You gave us all quite a scare."

"But Hester was right. It was worth it, Charles," Melissa said, glowing. "Look at my baby. Isn't he beautiful?"

Charles looked at the sleeping baby. He was a big, healthy-looking boy with an olive complexion and black hair, physical traits he had to have inherited from his father. Missy was fair and blond. So were Pam and George and both of Melissa's brothers.

"He's handsome, all right." *Just like his father was.*

"Did you see the reporters, Charles?" Melissa said, changing the subject, as if sensing that everyone was thinking about Brad, but no one wanted to mention him.

"Yes. They're chomping at the bit for an interview, Melissa, and I think you should give them one."

"I do, too," Melissa quickly agreed. "You're thinking what I'm thinking, aren't you? That it would be a great way to publicize Missy's Kid Cuisine."

"Absolutely. So, if you're up to it, I'd schedule the interview for as soon as possible. I imagine the newsworthy potential for human-interest stories is pretty short."

"I told Rena, the nurse, to have the reporters call me in the morning, then I'll see them right after lunch. I should be rested and presentable by then." She looked past Charles at Pam. "Mom, you'll have to bring me some makeup."

"Of course," Pam answered, as if that was understood.

Charles didn't think the makeup was necessary, but kept his opinion to himself.

"I'll tell them that I want all three networks sharing time during one single interview," Melissa continued, "not three separate interviews."

"That's smart," Charles said. "Three interviews might be too exhausting."

"I can't imagine it taking too long, though. I'm sure it's just going to be a quicky tag-on to the real news."

"Just make sure you mention Missy's Kid Cuisine," her father piped up. "You deserve something tangible from this elevator fiasco. I've half a mind to sue the hospital.''

''They were just trying to supply power and resources where it was needed most,'' Melissa reasoned. ''I'm sure they didn't realize how close I was to giving birth. And they couldn't anticipate the complications I developed. And when they did, they got the elevator moving.'' She smiled down at the baby. ''Besides, what's more tangible than what I'm holding in my arms? Even if I wasn't going to get the chance to plug my product on local TV, I feel more than compensated.''

''What are you going to name him?'' Charles asked. If she said she was naming him Brad Junior, he'd have a better inkling of where things stood.

Melissa turned and looked out the window. ''I don't know yet. I have an idea, but I haven't decided if it's a good one,'' she answered evasively.

The baby stirred and Melissa turned again to look down at him. ''He's finally waking up, the sleepy head. And he'll be hungry. It's a good thing they didn't give me any pain medications, otherwise I'd have to give him a bottle.''

So, she was breast-feeding. This was Charles's cue to vacate the premises. As much as he'd like to stay, he didn't have the right.

''I'm going to go now, Melissa,'' he announced. ''Sleep well tonight.''

''Charles, before you go… I'm guessing the reporters will want to interview you, too. You don't have a business to promote, but are you interested in being my sidekick in this little media circus?''

Melissa spoke lightly, but Charles sensed she would appreciate his presence during the interview.

He wasn't all that keen on the idea of appearing on television, but he'd do it for Melissa. Besides, it meant he'd be seeing her again, soon.

"Sure. I guess so. Call me and let me know when to be here."

She nodded, smiled. "I will. Kiss the kids for me." Mention of the children seemed to jolt Melissa. "Oh! You're out of a nanny, Charles! And your *paper!* Will you get it done in time with all this extra stuff I've managed to throw your way? Oh, poor Charles! You hired me to help make your life easier, not complicate it."

"Don't worry. Lily can help out till I get another nanny. And Mrs. Butters will be back Saturday, remember? We'll be okay. Don't worry about us. You've got someone else depending on you now."

Melissa nodded. "Yes, but—"

Melissa was about to blurt out that she *wanted* to worry about Charles and Christopher and Sarah and Daniel. She hadn't been doing it for very long, but it felt natural and good. She had no right, she knew, but she was jealous of anyone taking her place, even if it was only for two more days.

Hiding her feelings, she just smiled and shook her head, leaving her unfinished sentence dangling in the air. "Okay. I'll talk to you tomorrow, Charles. Good night."

He said, "Good night," and with one last, lingering, enigmatic look, he was gone.

"So, how long has *this* been going on?" her father inquired as soon as the door had closed behind Charles.

Melissa blushed. "What do you mean, Dad?"

"You and the professor. It's obvious you've got a thing for each other."

"*Dad.*"

"Your father's right, Melissa," her mother quickly corroborated. "I know it's still early in the game, but it's obvious that Charles cares for you. And that you have feelings for him. I hope this means you've told him the truth about Brad?"

George scowled. "What truth? That he was a bum? Or that he was a bastard?"

"*George!*" Pam remonstrated. "Not in the presence of your grandchild!"

George shrugged, unrepentant. "Why not? He doesn't understand me. And, thank God, he won't have to find out firsthand what a jerk his father is." He pursed his lips and looked consideringly at Melissa. "Does Charles know what a jerk Brad is?"

"Daddy, Charles thinks Brad is dead!" Melissa blurted out.

George looked understandably perplexed. "Where did he get that impression?"

"From me," Melissa admitted. "And don't ask me why I'd do such a stupid thing. I've regretted it from day one."

"She didn't know at the time that Charles actually *had* lost his spouse in a car accident," Pam explained. "And when Melissa found out, she felt even worse for lying."

George scowled at Pam. "You knew about this?"

Pam nodded. "Yes."

"Why didn't you advise your daughter to fess up?"

Pam shrugged. "George, I did."

George shook his head. "Okay. I could ask a thousand questions…but I won't. I'll just ask one. Why didn't you do what your mother advised? Why haven't you set that man straight on what's really going on in your life? He seems like a decent guy. He doesn't deserve to be lied to.''

Melissa blinked back tears. Her father wasn't yelling, or even speaking much above a whisper. But he was disappointed in her, and that hurt.

''To tell you the truth, Dad, I've been miserable keeping this secret. More and more as each day passed. But I was afraid to tell him before my five days working as his nanny was up. I loved taking care of his children. I enjoyed his company. I didn't want to create an awkwardness when things were so pleasant and nice. So family-like.'' She sighed, then ended miserably, ''I just didn't want to screw things up before I absolutely had to.''

George put his hand on Melissa's shoulder. ''I can understand you wanting something you never had with Brad. I understand…but now you absolutely have to tell him the truth. Before the interview, Missy. Before one of those reporters asks about your husband. I don't think you're prepared to lie on television and tell the whole state of Utah that your husband is dead, are you? Brad's mother is gone, and I suppose his father is still somewhere in south Florida, but as hard as it is to believe, Brad still has friends in this state. They might be shocked to hear he's passed on. Did you think about all that?''

Melissa obviously had not thought of all that. For the last hour she'd thought only of her baby, the closeness she'd shared with Charles, the gratitude she felt toward him for being there and for being everything she needed, and of her own good fortune in surviving a difficult birth. It had made her hopeful and impulsive. She'd decided on doing the interview before thinking it through.

"I can cancel the interview," she murmured.

"Why?" George challenged. "So you can postpone telling Charles the truth?"

Melissa knew he was right. She was stalling. She nodded and looked down at her baby, who was now starting to root at her hospital gown, obviously hungry for his first taste of mother's milk.

"After I set the time for the interview tomorrow, I'll call Charles and ask him to come to the hospital an hour early. I'll tell him then about Brad. And whatever happens, happens."

Shortly after this announcement, George and Pam kissed their daughter and their new grandson goodbye. They told her to expect phone calls from her brothers in the morning, both of whom had been alarmed and then relieved when Pam was finally able to get through on the busy phone lines to tell them about her history-making elevator experience. They left, smiling fondly at her as they waved themselves out the door.

Melissa just hoped Charles would be as forgiving of her as her parents were...although that was probably too much to ask. Just after her parents left, Rena returned.

"Good, I'm glad you're back, Rena," Melissa said, as she shifted the front of her gown to bare a breast. "He's hungry and I'm ready to feed him, but I'm not sure if I know how to do this."

"Well, your baby knows what to do. Just put a nipple close to his mouth and watch what happens, Melissa," Rena assured her.

Melissa brought the baby close to her breast and he eagerly latched on to her nipple, just as Rena said he would. As he tugged and sucked, Melissa's heart felt as if it would burst with love.

"How...how do I know he's getting anything?" she asked anxiously, watching his little mouth working away.

"Listen... Can you hear him swallowing?"

Melissa listened. Yes! He *was* swallowing.

"He's actually eating, Rena. And I'm actually feeding him!" Melissa marveled.

Rena chuckled. "Honey, he's a natural. And so are you. I'm sure the two of you are going to get along just fine."

Melissa hoped so, because it might always be just the two of them. She bit her lip and wondered if Charles had remembered to kiss the kids for her. It might be the last time he'd ever consent to do so.

Chapter Eight

"…and the baby came out of Melissa's tummy while we were still on the elevator. Since they have special rooms in the hospital for mommies who are having babies, lots of people thought that Melissa having a baby in a weird place like an elevator should be told on the television news. And since I was with Melissa when the baby was born, they want to talk to me, too."

Christopher sat at the kitchen table and stared at his father with a thoughtful expression. Charles could feel the sweat beading on his upper lip. He was hoping that his son wouldn't inquire exactly how a baby came out of a mommy's tummy, but if he did, he'd have to think of some way of explaining it without giving Christopher more information than he needed or wanted. Charles already felt like he was talking down to him. The kid was too darn smart for his own good *and* Charles's comfort!

Thank goodness, Sarah had been satisfied with the simple explanation that Melissa had gone to the hospital to have her baby, probably thinking it was a sort of warehouse full of babies to be picked up by ladies with fat tummies. After breakfast, she and

Daniel had gone into the family room and were, from the sounds of things, emptying the toy chest of every single item inside.

Daniel, of course, was happily oblivious, except for occasionally inquiring during breakfast, with a mouthful of Cheerios, "Where's M'lissa?"

"Is Melissa coming back?" Christopher finally asked.

Charles breathed a silent prayer of thanks that they'd perhaps gone beyond the medical questions.

"Not to take care of you guys, sport," Charles answered, ruffling Christopher's hair. "She's going to be in the hospital for a couple of days, then she'll go home to her own place to take care of her new baby. In the meantime, I'll take care of you day and night till Mrs. Butters gets back. Except for an hour or two this afternoon, that is. I'll need to get a baby-sitter for you while I go to the hospital for the interview."

Christopher nodded soberly, as if it was the answer he had expected, but was hoping for something different. "I like Mrs. Butters a whole lot, but I like Melissa, too. Will we ever see her again?"

Charles considered how best to answer this question. If it was up to him, you bet they'd see her again! But he still wasn't sure how it was all going to play out. Melissa had called that morning with the time of the interview, but she'd also asked him to come to the hospital an hour or so earlier...so they could talk about something *important*.

Charles knew the fact that Melissa wanted to discuss something important with him could either be a good sign or a bad sign about where their relationship was heading. He was very nervous and had a hard time thinking about much else. But Christopher still needed his question answered. Charles decided just to be as honest with him as possible.

"I don't know if we'll see much of Melissa anymore, now that she's no longer our temporary nanny, but I *think* we will. I *hope* so, anyway, and I guess you hope so, too."

Christopher nodded vigorously. "We'll have to invite her over. Or go see her and the baby at her house, like we go see Aunt Lily and her kids."

"Sounds like a plan, Christopher," Charles said, then glanced at his watch. He still had to call around to get a babysitter. But Christopher wasn't through.

"Dad?"

"Yeah?"

"Melissa said she was a missus. So that means she's married, right?"

"Well, yes, she *was* married, but—"

"So the baby has a dad, right?"

Charles had assumed that Christopher knew Melissa's husband was dead, but he'd been playing with his ball during that particular discussion after Melissa first arrived, so perhaps he hadn't been paying attention. And Melissa would never have brought up the subject voluntarily.

"All babies have dads, Christopher," Charles began carefully. Christopher understood death. He'd been very young when Annette died, and probably had only vague memories of her, but he knew he was different than most children because he was minus a mommy. Would Christopher be upset that this baby was minus a daddy?

"But you took Melissa to the hospital," Christopher continued, while Charles still hesitated. "Why didn't the baby's dad do that?"

Charles sighed. "Christopher, Melissa was married to a man named Brad. I knew him once—not very well, but a little—just like I knew Melissa many years ago. They got married right after they finished going to high school. But a few months ago—"

Charles stopped when he realized he didn't even know exactly when Brad died. Or if he should tell Christopher it had happened because of a car accident, just like his mother. He didn't want the poor kid getting paranoid about car accidents!

"Did they get a d'vorce?"

Charles stared into the wide, curious, innocent eyes of his four-year-old son and felt sad that he even knew and understood the word *divorce*. But then, Christopher had a few friends with no daddies, or two daddies, or sometimes two mommies, et cetera, and he'd asked Charles a couple of months ago to explain why this happened.

"No, they didn't divorce." He took a deep breath. "Christopher, Melissa's husband died in a car crash."

Christopher's eyes got bigger, more sober. "Oh."

"But that doesn't mean the baby will never have a dad," Charles pointed out to lessen the blow. "Someday Melissa might get married again and her new husband will be the baby's dad."

Christopher nodded consideringly.

"But even if Melissa never marries again, she'll be such a good mom to the baby, he'll be okay even without a dad," Charles added, striving to cover all the bases.

Christopher continued to nod, then suddenly

looked up, his eyes bright with some new thought or idea or question to ask. Charles held his breath, hoping he was up for whatever came out of Christopher's mouth next.

"I have a good idea," Christopher announced. "Since we don't have a mom, and Melissa's baby doesn't have a dad, why don't you and Melissa get married and then we'll have a mom, and the baby will have a dad?"

Charles could kick himself. He should have seen this coming from a mile off. But he wasn't sure he could have thwarted Christopher's reasoning that brought him to this "simple" conclusion, even if he *had* seen it coming.

"Christopher—"

"Then we can keep Mrs. Butters as our nanny, and have Melissa for our *mom!*" Christopher's enthusiasm was obviously growing the longer he considered this idea.

"But before two people can become husband and wife, they—"

"Wouldn't you like to have Melissa around all the time, Dad? And you'd be the baby's dad! Wouldn't you like that?"

Charles would like that very much. He'd been thinking that he'd like to be the father of Melissa's baby almost since the day she'd shown up on his doorstep. Having such feelings develop so strongly and so quickly was scary. But time would tell if they were as lasting and true as he thought they were. Only Christopher didn't want to wait and see, or even get Melissa's opinion of this great plan of his. He wanted a new mom and a new brother *right now!*

"All right, Christopher, I need you to understand

something,'' Charles began, but was interrupted by the doorbell ringing. Christopher was immediately on his feet and running into the living room. Charles had no choice but to follow him.

It was only eight-thirty, so Charles couldn't imagine who was at the door...except possibly Lily. As he walked through the living room, he practiced his ''thanks, but no thanks'' speech, because if it was Lily she'd probably come over to babysit or take the kids off on some excursion, even though he'd told her not to. Damn, that girl was stubborn!

He'd mentioned the interview last night when he came home from the hospital, but had explained that he was going to cancel his classes for the day— something he never did, so didn't feel too badly about—and call a neighborhood girl or a student to babysit while he was gone for the necessary hour or two. He didn't want Lily babysitting again because he felt as if she'd done more than her share of helping out during the last crazy three days.

Christopher opened the door. Sure enough, it was Lily. Her three youngsters flew past Charles and into the house at the speed of light, taking Christopher with them and leaving Charles alone with his sister. For some reason, her hair looked more like a disheveled haystack than usual, but he couldn't be sure whether it was because she was rushed and frazzled and hadn't had time to fuss with her hair, or because she'd actually put *extra* time into her styling routine that morning. He wasn't going to ask.

''Hello, Lily,'' he growled. ''What are you doing here?''

''Geez, Charles, what charm school did you go to? So when's the interview?''

"You don't waste time on opening chitchat and small talk, do you?"

"You didn't, so why should I? Besides, I'm your sister, Charles, not your dentist. I already know too much about you. Now...back to business. Did Melissa call?"

Charles stepped reluctantly aside and Lily walked in, heading straight for the sofa. She sat down, folding her long, tanned legs under her. From the family room, the commotion of six children was already reaching a crescendo.

"Yes, Melissa called," Charles answered, still standing. He paused, then added, "She wants me to come up there an hour earlier, though."

"Aha!" Lily exclaimed triumphantly.

Charles frowned. "What's the 'aha' for?"

"She wants to talk to you about something important, right?"

Charles shrugged. "Yeah. So, how did you know that?"

"I'm a woman, Charles." She pointed to her eyes. "I *see* things." She pointed to her ears. "I *hear* things. I come to conclusions. You're a man, and because of inherent genetic shortcomings, you are unable to come to the same correct conclusions as quickly and easily as I can."

Charles shook his head and sighed. "I know you mean well, Lily, but I don't want to hear your conclusions. I don't want to have any expectations about this talk with Melissa—"

"Aha!" she shouted again. "So, you *do* care. But you don't want to get your hopes up."

Charles did not want to have this conversation with Lily. He was taking this day a minute and an hour at a time. He truly did not want to think ahead and come up with his own conclusions, or conclusions influenced by his sister's biased and romantic point of view. In other words, she was right...he didn't want to get his hopes up.

"I need to make some phone calls, Lily," he said, smiling apologetically, hoping to elicit some understanding and end the conversation without offending her.

Lily raised a brow. "Just as I thought. You don't have a babysitter yet, do you?"

"I've been pretty busy this morning," Charles explained impatiently. "What with all Christopher's questions about babies and daddies and everything else you can imagine."

Lily grinned and nodded understandingly. "I can only imagine. I hope you didn't have to use the word *uterus?*"

"No, it didn't get that far, thank goodness. But I had to deal with some other pretty difficult words like *car accident, death* and *divorce.*"

Lily sobered. "Oh. He didn't know Melissa is a widow?"

"I guess he didn't hear when she told me that first day, and neither I nor Melissa ever brought up the subject again. Incredibly, considering Christopher's propensity for asking questions, inquiring about the baby's father didn't occur to him till this morning." Charles turned and headed toward the kitchen. "But I've got calls to make."

Lily got up and followed him. "Charles, why are you being so stubborn? You know I'm here to watch the kids."

"You've given up too much of your time already this week, Lily. I don't want to burden you."

Lily laughed. "Charles, *hello.* Remember, I offered to watch the kids for the whole week, only you wouldn't let me? I *love* watching them. I'm watching my own kids anyway, and they have a blast together, so why are you being so...so...*Charles?* How could you think for even a second that playing with my niece and nephews would be a burden! You'd do the same for me, Charlie Chuckle-head!"

Charles couldn't help it. He turned around and laughed out loud, filled with affection for his sister. "You haven't called me that since we were kids."

She grinned, abashed. "Not when you could actually hear me," she admitted.

Charles shook his head, smiling. "You're as stubborn as I am."

"Which frequently gets us into these kinds of arguments. For once, Charles, just let me have my way."

"'For once,' she says," he muttered. "You get your way most of the time."

She gloated and he smiled at her for a couple of minutes, then he said, "Listen, I'll make a deal with you. I'll let you babysit for me today if you promise to go away for a weekend with Josh real soon and let *me* watch all the kids."

Lily laughed and raised a skeptical brow. "You have no idea what you're getting yourself into, Charles, but if that's the only way I'll get you to let me babysit, you've got a deal."

ON THE WAY to the hospital, Charles wondered if he'd chosen the right clothes to wear for the interview. He figured Melissa wouldn't be in hospital garb, that her mother would bring something from home for her to wear. But would it be regular clothing or a nice robe? Melissa was still recovering from her difficult birth and the extra stuff they'd had to do to stop her bleeding, so he doubted she'd be in anything very fitted or constricting.

Well, whatever she wore, she'd look beautiful.

He'd finally chosen a navy sport jacket and nice gray slacks. Dressy casual. And all done in plenty of time to get to the hospital an hour before the scheduled interview. But Sarah had fallen down in the family room and scraped her chin on the edge of a coffee table five minutes before his planned departure, and it had taken him fifteen minutes of hugging and kissing and three Band-Aids to console her. As long as her daddy was around, Sarah didn't want anyone else kissing her boo-boos, and now he was running late.

Along Thirteenth East, just five minutes from the hospital, he was applying too much pedal to the metal and he was pulled over by a policeman.

Charles considered telling the policeman that he was late for a television interview about helping a woman give birth in an elevator, but decided it sounded desperate and unbelievable. Besides, the policeman seemed grouchy, even though Charles was only going seven miles per hour above the thirty miles per hour speed limit on a non-residential road that he knew people routinely traversed at forty miles per hour! Maybe the heat was getting to the police force, just as it was getting to just about everyone else in the valley. It was another scorcher, the temperature expected to exceed 105 for an unprecedented sixth day in a row, capturing for Salt Lake City a whole lot of national news coverage.

Oh, well, who knew why the police officer was a grouch? Besides, Charles *had* been speeding, so it was his own fault he'd been pulled over in the first place.

But what was the holdup? The policeman had taken Charles's driver's license and was sitting in his patrol car, probably checking him out on the computer. Since Charles hadn't had a ticket in over five years, he wondered what could possibly be taking so long.

Finally the policeman sauntered back to Charles's car and bent down to peer at him through the window. "I'm going to let you off with a warning this time, Mr. Avery. But from now on, watch your speed along here, okay?"

Although surprised, Charles couldn't care less about being spared a ticket, but he was elated that the policeman was finally letting him go. "Thanks, officer," he said gratefully.

The officer attempted a sort of grumpy smile, then drawled, "Have a nice day," and returned to his patrol car.

Charles had lost another twenty minutes of precious time, but he didn't dare speed now, so carefully stayed within the speed limit till he pulled into the University Hospital parking lot. It took him another five minutes to find a parking spot, and by the time he was pressing the elevator button to the sixth floor, it was twelve-forty. There were only twenty minutes left before the interview and Charles was resigned to the fact that he and Melissa were probably going to have to postpone their "important" conversation till after the interview.

As he approached Melissa's hospital room, he saw a lot of activity in the hallway just outside her door. Equipment, reporter-types in suits, curious hospital staff.

He squeezed his way into the room and saw Melissa in the midst of a crowd, having her nose dotted with a powder puff. She was wearing a rose-colored robe, her shiny hair neatly combed and styled, resting on her shoulders. As he'd expected, she looked beautiful. When she saw him, she exclaimed, "Charles!"

Gratified, he went immediately to her bedside. She grasped his hand and looked up at him, but the expression in her eyes was anxious. "Where have you been, Charles?"

"I'm sorry, Melissa. Sarah had an accident just before I left the house and—"

"Is she okay?"

"She's okay. It was just a scrape. But then on the way over here, I was pulled over for speeding and—"

"Oh, it doesn't matter anyway," Melissa interrupted, biting her lip and looking around distractedly at all the people in the room. "I had no idea how long it took to set up for one of these things! Even if you'd been on time, we wouldn't have had a chance to talk."

Charles got accidentally bumped from behind. "It is kind of chaotic in here."

"There's national media here, too," Melissa said, her voice a mix of wonder and worry.

"Wow!" Charles squeezed her hand. "That's

good, isn't it? You'll get even more publicity for your company.''

"Yes, unless they edit it out," Melissa agreed cautiously.

"But mentioning Missy's Kid Cuisine is part of the deal, isn't it?"

Melissa nodded. "Yes, but I don't know…"

"You've just got stage fright, Melissa."

When Melissa didn't respond, but continued to look anxious, Charles tried changing the subject. "Where's the baby?"

"I told them to keep the baby in the nursery till just before the shoot. Mom and Dad are with him. They're going to bring him in when it's time, and I told the news people that I didn't want a bunch of noise and confusion scaring him. They'd better keep their word!"

Charles was alarmed by the level of stress in her voice. "Melissa, this is a great opportunity for you. In fact, it's getting better by the minute. But if you're not feeling well enough, or if you've got any second thoughts at all, I'll send all these people packing…right now."

She looked up at him, her eyes glistening. "You would, wouldn't you? You're such a nice guy, Charles, but you're firm and strong, too."

Charles supposed he should feel flattered by this description of him, but the sad tone of her voice was setting off alarms inside him. He had this uneasy feeling that something bad was about to happen.

"I want to do this interview, Charles, and I'm truly feeling fine…physically. But I need to tell you something," she continued urgently. "Something that can't wait till after the interview."

He squeezed her hand, trying to reassure her…and himself. "What could you possibly need to tell me that can't wait a few minutes? Don't worry. I'll stay as long as you want after the interview. Lily's with the kids and she's—"

"No." Melissa's tone was determined, abrupt. "By then it might be too late."

Charles laughed uneasily. "What do you mean?"

"Professor Avery? Professor Avery!"

Charles ignored whoever was trying to get his attention and bent closer to Melissa. "What's wrong, Melissa? What do you need to tell me?"

Some woman jostled Charles's elbow, insisting, "We need to do some makeup, Professor Avery."

"Melissa…*tell me.*" Charles prompted, bending closer still.

Melissa's bottom lip trembled. She whispered, "It's about Brad. He's—"

Her eyes widened as her gaze abruptly shifted to a point beyond Charles's shoulder.

Charles shook his head, puzzled. "He's what, Melissa?"

"He's… He's… Oh, my God, he's *here!*"

Charles wasn't sure he'd heard right. Brad was *there?* How? In spirit? Brad couldn't be there. He was dead. Was Melissa hallucinating?

Melissa's eyes fluttered shut, then opened, then stared past Charles's shoulder again. *"Oh my God,"* she repeated.

Charles straightened up and turned around, looking for whatever apparition Melissa thought she saw.

But what he saw was no ghost. Just outside the door, big as life, in the flesh, stood Brad Baxter. An older version of the high-school jock Charles remembered, a little heavier, but the same man. Tall, black-haired, blue-eyed, and still exuding a swaggering physicality.

As Charles watched numbly, disbelieving, Brad smiled and waved at Melissa—who didn't wave back—then shifted his gaze to Charles. His eyes narrowed and the corners of his mouth slipped abruptly down. It looked like Brad Baxter was about as pleased to see Charles as Charles was to see him.

Only Charles had the added disadvantage of having received the biggest and most unpleasant surprise of his life.

Melissa was surrounded by noise and confusion. People were telling her what to do, what to expect. They were adjusting her pillows, the lights, her bangs. She was looking at her ex-husband, standing just outside the door, and feeling shock, horror and disgust at his sudden appearance.

But what registered the most with Melissa was the sensation of Charles slowly but firmly pulling his fingers free of her trembling hold on them. He was withdrawing from her. He had been lied to, and now he knew Brad was very much alive! But worse still, he *didn't* know that she and Brad were divorced!

She had to tell him! She had to let him know that Brad wasn't welcome there, hadn't been expected. That they'd agreed that she would raise the baby without him. In fact, the divorce papers included a custody agreement. Melissa had sued for and been granted sole custody of their unborn child, and she'd released Brad of any responsibility for child support, an arrangement he was completely happy with. He hadn't wanted to be a father, so she'd never dreamed he'd show up like this. Unless he had an ulterior motive...

"Charles, listen—"

But Charles had moved away from the bed, dragged off by the tenacious makeup technician who had been trying to get his attention for some time. She'd pulled him into a corner of the room and was patting his face with a little powder. Melissa heard the technician, who was an attractive young woman, teasing Charles, telling him "not to look so glum." After a little more teasing and laughing, the technician finally had Charles smiling. Melissa wasn't sure if she was happy or sad that the technician had succeeded in making Charles smile. It looked more than a little forced, but it was still a smile, and *she* wanted to make him smile by telling him that she was divorced! D-I-V-O-R-C-E-D, *divorced!*

But that might not be enough. She still had to explain why she'd lied about Brad being dead.

Brad.

Melissa braved another glance at the door. He was still standing there among other onlookers, soberly watching her. Even though he'd probably been told to stay back and out of the way, she had a horrible feeling he might jostle and force his way through the crowd of reporters, cameramen and equipment, announce he was the baby's father and claim a place by her side. He'd love the attention.

Melissa motioned to a young, red-headed nurse, standing in the background keeping an eye on things. She approached and Melissa whispered in her ear. "See that man at the door?"

The nurse nodded, smiled. "The real good-looking one with black hair?"

Melissa sighed. "Yeah, that one. Would you please make sure he doesn't come near me?"

The nurse looked startled. "Oh. Why?"

"He's my ex-husband and he isn't supposed to be here. I don't want him to ruin this interview." That wasn't true, though. What she was really concerned about was that he'd ruin any chance she had left of making things right with Charles.

The nurse stared at Brad, who noticed he was the object of her attention and threw her one of his abashed, boy-next-door, flirtatious grins. Melissa could see the nurse reacting to Brad—flattered and self-conscious, blushing, eyelashes fluttering—as women always did.

"Gee, are you sure he'd be a problem? He looks perfectly harmless and nice to me."

"Trust me, he'd be a problem. More to the point, *I'd* be a problem if he came anywhere near me."

Melissa's tone was emphatic enough and serious enough to interrupt the nurse's fascination with Brad. She dragged her gaze back to Melissa and said, "Well, even if he *is* perfectly harmless, *you* don't think so and we don't want you getting upset, Mrs. Baxter."

"It's Ms. Richardson," Melissa corrected.

"But your chart says your name is—"

"Never mind."

"Do you want me to call security and have him removed from the area?"

"No, I don't want attention drawn to him, or to cause a commotion of any kind. Especially with all these reporters and cameras here. Please, just don't let him near me, okay? I'm sure you can find a way to keep him occupied and outside this room," Melissa hinted.

The nurse nodded and went immediately to do her duty, although Melissa suspected the nurse wasn't exactly dreading the task of keeping Brad occupied. He still had the looks and outward charm to wow the women.

Eventually, the makeup technician released Charles and he was directed to stand by the bed. Charles looked her way and Melissa smiled encouragingly, apologetically, but he didn't smile back. He did, however, move to stand beside the bed.

"Kelso, get the baby in here," shouted one of the television crew. "We're shooting this in three minutes."

It was now or never, so Melissa grabbed Charles's hand again...only this time his fingers didn't automatically curl around hers. They were stiff and cool.

"Charles," she whispered. "Please listen to me."

He looked down at her, his expression neutral and unencouraging.

She swallowed hard. "We don't have to do this interview, you know. You probably don't want to anymore and I understand completely. Send them away and we'll talk."

"It's too late, Melissa," Charles answered, his tone as expressionless as his face. Did his words have a double meaning? "After all this preparation, it wouldn't be fair to the networks, and they wouldn't take kindly to an abrupt dismissal. Besides, you need to do this to advertise your business."

"But that's not as important to me as—"

As you.

He just stared at her, politely waiting for her to

finish, she supposed. She couldn't. But she *could* say what she'd been trying to say all along.

"Brad and I are divorced, Charles," she blurted, grateful that no one around her was paying attention to them at the moment, but determined finally to speak even if she was heard by everyone in the room. "I…I lied to you about him…him being dead because—"

"Here's the baby," someone shouted, interrupting Melissa's stammered attempt to explain. Among a chorus of "oohs and aahs" Melissa's mother and father wended their way through the crowd. Both grandparents beamed as Pam placed the baby in Melissa's arms.

"Honey, you look pale and nervous," Pam whispered as she bent close to her ear. "What's wrong? You told Charles, didn't you? Didn't he take it well?"

But Melissa had no time to reply. All of the lights were turned on, all of the cameras were trained on Melissa and her baby and the grave, silent man standing beside her. Someone started a countdown, Melissa and Charles were ordered to smile, and suddenly they were on the air.

Chapter Nine

Charles's mind was whirling. There was a lot to take in all at once. First Brad—the dead husband of the woman he was falling in love with—shows up. He briefly considered the possibility that Melissa had really thought Brad was dead and had been as shocked as he was to see him standing at the door to the hospital room…a dead man come to life again, kind of like a scene from a Hitchcock movie! But Charles almost instantly dismissed that idea. Melissa didn't scream or faint. She hadn't reacted as though she'd seen a ghost at all. Her reaction was more a mixture of shocked dismay and guilt.

He'd had no alternative but to conclude that she'd lied to him…then later she'd actually admitted to it.

And what a cruel lie! She had no idea how horrible it was to lose your marriage partner in a terrible accident. It wasn't something you ''pretended'' to have happened for any reason that Charles could imagine.

So why *had* she done it? While the makeup technician powdered his face and chatted him up, Charles considered all the possible answers to this question. He came up with nothing that made him feel one bit better.

Another sobering possibility was that Melissa was still married to Brad, and Charles had been falling in love with a married woman! Indications were that it wasn't a happy or a successful marriage, but maybe they were just separated and trying to work out differences. Anything was possible. Trouble was, Charles had no way of knowing the real truth of the matter. Obviously Melissa had been hiding secrets from him all week.

By the time he'd been released by the makeup technician and ordered back to Melissa's side, Charles had decided to make the best of the present situation. If he stalked out of the room, leaving Melissa in the lurch and forced to make some sort of explanation for his hasty departure, it would be quite stressful for her and might ruin the whole interview. He still wanted her to get some benefit from having delivered a baby in an elevator, and free publicity for her new business seemed as close to fair compensation as it was going to get.

Then, when Melissa grabbed his hand and looked at him so urgently, so shame-faced and earnest, he'd felt his heart melting. But he'd tried to appear unfazed. He wasn't ready to put his heart out there to be hammered again.

Charles was initially relieved to hear that Melissa and Brad were divorced, but her quick, stammered attempt to explain why she'd lied about being a widow had been cut short, leaving him still in the dark. What reasonable explanation could she have?

"When you hired Ms. Richardson as your nanny, did you ever expect you'd be helping her deliver her baby in an elevator?"

Charles was forced to set aside the troubling

thoughts that were overwhelming him. The interview had begun and questions from the reporters, initially directed to Melissa, were now being lobbed his way. The question was a dumb one—who, except a psychic, could anticipate being a fill-in birth coach in an elevator?—but he smiled and answered, "No, of course not. She did appear to be ready to burst when she showed up on my doorstep that first day—"

Good-natured laughter, amused chuckles.

"—but she thought she had a couple more weeks before the baby's birth, so I thought I was safe." Half for effect, half because he couldn't help himself, Charles looked down at Melissa and smiled, dropping his hand to her shoulder for a gentle, reassuring squeeze. "But I'm glad I was there...even though I had to miss a meteor shower."

While the reporters emitted various noises of approval, Melissa looked up at him, smiled uncertainly, and put her hand over his. Judging by the whirring of cameras and the number of flashbulbs going off, the reporters loved this touching little tableau. Charles figured it would definitely help promote Melissa's business. He answered a few more questions about the actual events that had taken place in the elevator, during which he eased his hand off Melissa's shoulder and out from under her fingers.

"It must have been pretty scary when Ms. Richardson fainted," a reporter suggested, obviously wanting to draw out as much emotion as possible.

Charles answered truthfully. "It was definitely scary. I...we didn't know if Melissa was going to make it or not."

"Melissa said you were in high school together.

Were you sweethearts?'' a reporter in the back piped up.

"No," Charles quickly answered. "We were friends." Not even that, really, he amended to himself. And now he had no idea what they were to each other.

"You're not married, right, Ms. Richardson?"

"Right," Melissa answered with a brittle but determined smile.

They waited, but when she didn't elaborate, another reporter asked, "Do you mind if I ask…are you widowed?"

"No, I'm not a widow," was Melissa's firm answer, still smiling determinedly. "I'm divorced. But I'll be raising the baby on my own. The father won't be involved."

Charles glanced up then, looking toward the door, half expecting Brad to barge in and announce that he was the father. But he didn't. He was standing in the hallway next to a red-headed nurse and paying almost as much attention to her as he was to the interview. But the nurse seemed to be doing all the talking. Maybe he had no choice.

"Maybe you won't be raising the baby alone," another female reporter speculated coyly. "You and Professor Avery seem to have become pretty close."

When Melissa made no comment—good grief, how could she?—Charles said, "An experience like this has the potential to bring a closeness between even complete strangers. It was pretty dramatic."

Sensing they weren't going to pry out any more comments that would support a romantic angle, the reporters finally asked Melissa about her baby-food business. Inwardly, Charles breathed a sigh of relief. Soon the interview would be over and he could go home. To think.

"I'M PLANNING ON OPENING my expanded store in a few weeks, as well as setting up an Internet site for ordering my baby food." Melissa smiled, and moved the blanket slightly away from her sleeping baby's face so the reporters could get a good picture of him. "But I've got something else to think about now, and my baby comes first. He's been awfully good, hasn't he?"

"What are you naming him?" a reporter from Channel Two inquired. "Is the name Charles in the running?"

Melissa laughed uneasily, not daring to look at Charles. "I haven't decided what to name him yet. But, yes, Charles is a very good name. I'll put it on my list."

The reporters finally wound down with a couple more pans of the three of them, carefully avoiding keeping the lights on the baby's face for more than a few seconds, and signed off.

Melissa accepted the thanks of the reporters and leaned back into her pillows. She was exhausted. Pretending to be bright and chipper when she really felt miserable inside had taken every ounce of energy she had.

The equipment was being dismantled and carted out and the roomful of people dispersing. Charles was shaking hands with reporters and, more or less, corralling them out the door. She couldn't see Brad anywhere, and she wondered where he'd gone. Back to California, she hoped, but she didn't think he'd come all that way just to turn around and go back without saying or doing whatever he came there to say or do. The red-headed nurse had disappeared, too.

Melissa closed her eyes…briefly, she thought. But when she opened them, the room was empty except for her mother and father. Charles was gone. Melissa felt her heart sink.

"What's wrong, Missy?" her father demanded, as her mother lifted the baby out of her arms. They both stared at her worriedly.

"Is it Charles?" her mother asked.

"Partly," Melissa admitted.

"What's the other part?" Pam prompted, as she tucked the blanket more securely around her little grandson's feet.

Melissa sighed and met their gazes squarely. "Brad's here."

Her father spun around, checking out the area for signs of his despised ex-son-in-law. "I didn't see him."

"He was out in the hall with a bunch of other people."

"Maybe it wasn't him," Pam suggested hopefully. "Maybe you just thought you saw him."

Melissa sighed. "Oh, it was him all right."

"What the hell is he doing here?" George growled.

"Probably just wanted to get on TV," Pam said.

"Well, if that's the case, why didn't he?" Melissa said tiredly. "He could have announced he was the baby's father at any time. I sent that cute red-headed nurse out there to distract him, but if he was really determined, Brad wouldn't have let her keep him out. Now if Rena had been the nurse I'd sent out there,

I could easily believe he'd been kept in the hall against his will.''

"Well, if he's not here for the glory of it all, why is he here?'' Pam asked, gently bouncing her grandson, who was finally stirring from his nap. "He didn't want to have anything to do with the baby. He gave you sole custody.''

"I don't know why he's here, Mom,'' Melissa answered. "But I'm sure we'll find out soon enough.''

"I wonder how he found out the baby was born,'' her father mused, rubbing the back of his neck.

"As you said, he still has lots of friends around here. Maybe one of them heard I'd given birth—in an elevator, no less—and called him,'' Melissa speculated.

"What happened with Charles?'' her father asked, moving on to the next subject.

Melissa shook her head. "If you don't mind, Dad, Mom, I don't think I have the energy to talk about Charles right now. It's too depressing…and I'm very tired. All I want to do is feed my baby, then take a nap. Okay?''

"Okay,'' Pam readily agreed, then handed Melissa her baby.

Holding him close to her, Melissa tried to block out all her worries and concentrate on the joy of being mother to such a beautiful, sweet little boy. No matter what happened, no matter what hassles Brad had in store for her, no matter whether or not Charles could forgive her, no matter if she stayed single the rest of her life…she and her baby were going to be just fine.

CHARLES DROVE AROUND for a couple of hours, thinking. Then he finally remembered that Lily was babysitting and turned toward home. When he came in from the garage, he could hear the children playing in the family room. Lily was in the kitchen, cooking something. It smelled like Sloppy Joes.

She turned, licking some tomato sauce off her fingers, when she heard him shut the door behind him. "Charles? Hey, how'd it go, bro?"

She met him halfway across the kitchen, but stopped in her tracks when she saw his face. "My God, what happened?"

Charles slumped down into a kitchen chair and gave her a grim little smile. "You'll never guess in a million years, Lily."

Lily plopped down in a chair across from him, clasped her hands together and placed them on the table in front of her. "I'm all ears, Charles."

"You mentioned your ears earlier today," Charles pointed out. "Your ears *and* your eyes, and how they alerted you to certain things that we men don't seem to hear or see till we're hit upside the head. But you didn't see this coming, I promise you that."

"Charles, for crying out loud, just tell me what happened!" Lily said impatiently.

"Melissa is not a widow."

"Say what?"

"Her husband is not dead."

"Brad Baxter...isn't dead?" Lily repeated slowly.

"You heard right."

"But Melissa told you—"

"Exactly."

"But why would she—?"

"I don't know."

Lily got up and started pacing the kitchen floor. ''Was she ever going to tell you?''

''I think that's why she wanted me to come to the hospital an hour before the interview. She probably knew the truth would come out when the reporters started asking a lot of questions, and unless she wanted to lie to a few million people who might be tuning into the national news, she had to tell the truth. I guess she didn't want me to hear it first during the interview.''

''Well, that was considerate of her,'' Lily muttered sarcastically. ''Hell, if I knew she was going to pull something like this...''

''But I got there late and she never got the chance to tell me,'' Charles continued.

Lily stopped pacing, her hands on her hips, a confused frown marring her usually smooth forehead. ''Well, then how *did* you find out?'' Before Charles could answer, Lily's head reared up and she exclaimed, ''Oh, no. Don't tell me! You found out *during* the interview?''

''No. It was before the interview. You see, Brad showed up at the hospital.''

Lily's mouth fell open. ''He showed up?''

''Yes. Just as Melissa was about to tell me he was alive, the proof was right there in the flesh.''

''You didn't think you were seeing a ghost?''

''No. But it was still a hell of a shock, I can tell you.''

''I'll bet.'' Lily dropped down into her chair again. ''What did Mr. Football Hero have to say for himself?''

''Nothing. He didn't even come into the room.'' Charles shrugged. ''After the interview, he just disappeared. Lily, I have no idea what's going on between him and Melissa.''

Lily patted Charles's hands, which were clasped together on top of the table. "I'm surprised you even went through with the interview, Charles.''

"Melissa needed the interview to advertise her baby food company. I wasn't going to bail on her at that point. She was so upset when she saw Brad, though, *she* was ready to bag it.''

"Only you convinced her not to, I suppose?'' Lily suggested with a knowing and affectionate smile. "Mad as hell at the girl, but still thinking of her welfare. Sir Charles, Knight in Shining Armor.''

Charles quickly said, "Look, I'm no knight. It just seemed a shame for those television crews to go home without a story after all their trouble, but more than that it would have been a real shame for Melissa to lose the opportunity to promote her business, free of charge. I just thought Melissa deserved *something* from giving birth in an elevator. She was very brave.''

"What does she deserve for lying to you, Charles? What kind of person tells someone—someone who lost their wife in a car accident—that they also lost their spouse in a car accident, and then it turns out to be a *big fat lie?*''

Charles stared at the kitchen table, picturing Melissa as she'd looked and acted that first day. "After thinking back over the past week, I remembered that Melissa told me that Brad had been killed in an accident *before* she knew that Annette had been killed the same way. In fact, when she first came from the nanny agency, she didn't even know my wife was dead. She thought Annette was in New Orleans.''

"Well, it *does* make me feel a little better that she didn't know about Annette," Lily conceded. "In fact, she probably felt awful when she found out."

"Probably. But why did she feel the need to tell such a lie in the first place? She started to explain it at the hospital, but there was too much going on and I didn't feel like sticking around to get the whole story."

"It's probably got something to do with her relationship with Brad," Lily mused. She looked up suddenly, as if just thinking of something important. "They *are* divorced, aren't they? 'Cause if she's still married, Charles, I say cut your losses and get away from her as fast as you can."

"She's divorced. But it's a moot point, really."

"Why is it 'moot,' Charles?" Lily asked him, exasperated. "And why don't you just speak plain English, please? How do you feel about Melissa, and what do you think will happen next?"

"I was falling in love with her," Charles answered truthfully. "But I was being careful, trying to go slowly, because I thought Melissa had recently lost her husband. She'd asked me not to mention him, so I assumed her feelings were still too new, too raw. But I thought I detected... I mean, I thought she might be growing a little fond of me, too."

"She was," Lily assured him.

"Then why didn't she tell me the truth about Brad?"

"Why don't you ask her?"

Charles shook his head. "Because I think it's best just to leave things as they are. Truth and trust are two of the most important aspects of a relationship. If she didn't tell the truth about Brad, maybe there are other secrets she's keeping. And, even though they're divorced, maybe she and Brad aren't...you know...finished.''

"And maybe they are," Lily countered.

Charles said nothing. He didn't want to think about Melissa any more. He was physically, mentally and emotionally drained and he still had a paper to finish for his lecture on Saturday. He pointedly changed the subject.

"You're cooking dinner kind of early, aren't you?"

Lily realized what he was doing but apparently wasn't ready to change the subject. "I wanted everything done so we could all sit down and watch the interview on the news at six. We can watch the Channel Five news, live, then watch tapes of Channel Two and Channel Four. I've got both your VCRs set to record. Josh is coming over straight from work. He's as eager to see his brother-in-law on television as the kids and I are."

"I wasn't going to watch even one version of the interview, much less three," Charles informed her.

"Oh, baloney, Charles. You know you will. You won't be able to resist."

"I have work to do."

"Watching all three interviews will probably take all of three minutes," Lily argued. "You know they relegate those stories to the tail-end of the news."

Charles sighed. She was right. No matter how upset he was with Melissa, no matter how conflicted his feelings, he wanted to see the interview...all three versions as edited by the three main national news networks.

God help him, he wanted to see Melissa one last time. Or maybe he should say, *three* last times.

"EVERYONE BE QUIET!" ordered Kent, Melissa's oldest brother. "They're talking about Salt Lake's heatwave. Melissa's story might be on next."

Melissa's nap had revived her energy, and then her brothers, Kent and Craig, Craig's wife, Sandy, and Melissa's parents had arrived together to help revive her spirits. They had the television on and were waiting for the showing of the interview during the six o'clock news.

Melissa's parents hadn't confided to the rest of the family the reason she was feeling a little low, but they hinted that she was feeling a bit overwhelmed at the idea of raising a baby as a single parent. They hadn't mentioned that Brad was in town, either, because Kent and Craig had been itching for a long time to put a permanent dent in Brad Baxter's nose. Pam and George didn't want a fistfight in the hospital as a follow-up story to the warm and fuzzy one that was going to be broadcast to the nation any minute now.

"I'm recording the other networks at home," Kent assured Melissa, as he held his new nephew in his arms.

Melissa smiled and nodded, but she wasn't sure she wanted to see all three versions, not to mention the longer, less edited versions that would be broadcast on the local networks. She wasn't even sure she was up to watching one!

The fact that Charles had left abruptly after the interview and she hadn't heard from him since weighed heavily on her. Even if he didn't understand or couldn't forgive her, even if she never saw him again afterward, Melissa wanted to explain why she'd lied to him.

It would be humbling admitting she hadn't been brave enough to expose her marriage—and her entire life the whole time she was married—as a failure. That she'd been naive and stupid. That she hadn't lived up to the promise of the girl she once was in high school.

But that's exactly what she needed and wanted to do.

If only Charles would give her the chance.

"It's starting!" exclaimed Sandy. "Oh, this is *so* exciting!"

The suited, distinguished, deep-voiced anchorman put on his genial persona to report this warmer, human-interest story.

"Salt Lake City's record-breaking, history-making heatwave and the resulting citywide blackout Wednesday night caused more than a smattering of traffic jams due to malfunctioning traffic signals. Five major hospitals in the area were left in the dark...but only for a few seconds until backup power sources generated enough energy for lights and lifesaving machines and equipment to resume functioning."

The anchorman's face grew even more sober.

"But at the University Hospital on the east bench overlooking the city, an unusual number of major surgeries were going on and critical patients were being kept alive by skilled surgeons, bypass machines and respirators. One hundred percent of the hospital's power was being diverted to these critical patients...leaving people stranded on the elevator."

The handsome anchorman quirked his brow.

"Normally this would not be a problem. People get stranded on elevators all the time...right? But Melissa Richardson—"

"Yay!" said Melissa. "He used my maiden name, just like I told them to!"

"—was in labor and riding the elevator to the sixth-floor maternity ward where a doctor was waiting to deliver her baby. But while the doctor was willing to wait...the baby wasn't. And when the elevator stalled, history was made."

After this lead-in, a voice-over narrated while various people were interviewed. Hester, the volunteer, Lana, the nurse, and Nathan, the orderly, all had a snippet of air time. Then the doctors who had fixed up Melissa after she was hurried into the delivery room made brief statements, stressing how urgent the situation had been.

"Goodness, I had no idea they interviewed so many people!" Melissa exclaimed, embarrassed and pleased at the same time.

Suddenly, there she was on television, holding her baby, with Charles standing beside the bed.

"That's the professor? Oh, he's *cute!*" Sandy purred.

Kent looked incredulous. "*That's* Charles Avery? He used to be a bean-pole with glasses."

Her father beamed. "You look beautiful on television, Missy."

"Yeah," quipped Craig. "You were smart to stay in bed for the interview, 'cause if the camera puts an extra ten pounds on you, it's hidden under the covers."

Pam "shushed" them because now the actual talking portions of the interview were being shown. Of course they edited out just about everything except the nice things she and Charles said to and about each other, purposely leaving the viewers with that warm, fuzzy feeling the networks were going for. They ended with a few questions and answers about Melissa's baby-food company, and a closeup—not of the baby's face—but of Charles's hand squeezing Melissa's shoulder and her hand reaching up to cover his.

The program returned to the New York news station and the handsome anchorman nodded and smiled. *"In crisis situations, heroes can be made of total strangers, or old friends, or a combination of the two. Even in such an unlikely place...as an elevator."*

The segment over, Pam flicked off the television. Everyone was completely quiet for a moment, then Craig, still irrepressibly mischievous at thirty-three, said in a singsong voice, "Missy's got a boyfriend."

Sandy echoed her husband's theme. "Hey, good going, Melissa! He's a catch. And you got him while you were pregnant, no less."

Melissa was blushing crimson. "Charles and I aren't a couple," she stressed. "We're just friends." *And maybe we're not even that anymore,* she said to herself.

"Looked like more than friends to me," Kent gave as his opinion.

"He was a little stiff, Melissa, but there was genuine feeling in his voice when he said he'd been worried that you wouldn't make it," Sandy added.

Melissa struggled to find the right words to fend off her well-meaning family. "Of course he was worried. He's a nice man. He would have been just as worried if he'd been in an elevator with a complete stranger who was bleeding to death.''

Her parents kept silent and the rest of them just looked at her dubiously.

''Really, guys,'' she insisted. ''In fact, I may have overstated the fact when I said Charles and I are friends. I've been working for him as his nanny for the past few days, and before that I hadn't seen him in thirteen years! So don't make a mountain out of a molehill, okay?''

Her brothers pursed their lips and raised their brows, keeping their mouths shut but still, obviously, holding on to their original opinion that Missy had a boyfriend. Well, when they didn't see Charles Avery again except on video tape, maybe then they'd believe her!

Melissa was glad when the phone rang. It was probably Kent's wife, Molly, checking to see when he was coming home. Her mother, closest to the phone, picked up the receiver.

''Hello? Oh… Yes, just a minute. She has some visitors, but I think *they're just leaving*.'' Pam rolled her eyes and motioned toward the door with a couple of head jerks.

Amusement and curiosity showed on everyone's faces as Pam handed the phone to Melissa. After all, why did they all have to leave just because she got a phone call?

''Who is it?'' Melissa whispered, her hand over the mouth piece.

Her mother smiled. ''It's Charles.''

Craig guffawed and left the room, throwing his sister a sly wink as he and Sandy departed. Kent kissed her on the cheek and whispered, "We'll give you a little privacy, Missy," then left, too. Her mother had taken the baby from Craig and said, "Your father and I will be down the hall at the nurses' station, showing off our grandson. We won't be leaving till I hear exactly what the professor had to say."

Finally, and suddenly, Melissa was alone in the room. Her heart was beating like a jackhammer and her mouth had gone as dry as the Sahara Desert.

She took a quick drink of water and prayed that Charles hadn't given up and hung up the phone.

"Hello?" she rasped.

"Melissa, is that you? You sound funny. Are you sick?"

She cleared her throat. "No, I'm fine. My throat's just a little dry, that's all."

There was a pause. A long pause. Melissa was about to say something when Charles finally spoke up. "Listen, I was just watching the interview on television."

"So was I," she said.

"You looked great, by the way."

Melissa smiled. "Well, so did you."

"I was watching Channel Five, and I flinched when he implied that I, along with the nurses and doctors who actually saved your life, was some kind of hero."

"But you were—"

"I wasn't. I just did what anyone would have done."

Melissa said nothing. He'd been *her* hero and she wasn't going to argue the point with him.

"It certainly wasn't heroic of me when I left today

without giving you a chance to explain about Brad,'' Charles continued, his words coming in a rush. ''I'm willing to listen now…that is, if you still want to talk.''

Melissa's heart swelled with hope and happiness. ''Of course, I still want to talk. Can't…can't we do it over the phone, though? Right now?''

''Let's talk in person, Melissa. How long are you going to be in the hospital?''

''I'm ready to get out of here right now, but they won't let me go home till Saturday. Can you come over then, to my apartment? Mom and Dad are driving me and the baby home around noon, so how does two o'clock sound? That should give me time to settle in a little and get rid of my doting parents.'' *Who are going to be joyous when they hear the gist of this conversation.*

''My lecture's at eleven o'clock. So, yeah, I should be able to swing by your place by two.''

Melissa pressed her palm against her cheek. ''Oh, Charles, I'm so embarrassed. I completely forgot about your lecture!''

''Who could blame you? It's been an eventful week.''

''Are you going to be ready?''

''Yeah, I'll be fine.''

''Well, good luck…although I doubt you'll need it.''

''Thanks. I'll see you Saturday.''

''Wait! You need my address.''

''Oh, yeah…''

''It's 1345 East Willow Wood Drive. Apartment number twelve, upstairs.''

''Great. Well, see you then.''

"Good night, Charles."

"Good night, Melissa."

Melissa hung up the phone, her hand lingering on the receiver almost like a caress. She couldn't quit smiling.

"Who was that?" came a well-remembered, most unwelcome voice from the door. "Your boyfriend?"

Melissa's smile vanished. She looked up and saw Brad lounging against the closed door to her room. Her first thought was that she was glad her parents had the baby. Her second thought was that she hoped she could get rid of Brad before they got back. Her third thought was that he looked different... Maybe it was because he had a serious expression on his face instead of the usual smug smile. Melissa felt the hairs standing up on the back of her neck.

"What are you doing here?" she asked him point blank. "And when are you leaving?"

"I'm here to see you, Missy. And my son. And I'm not leaving till you listen to all the reasons why you and I should get back together."

CHARLES HUNG UP the phone and turned around to find Lily and Josh standing at the study door.

"Did you listen to my entire conversation?" he inquired, pretending to be offended. But Lily wasn't fooled, and neither was Josh.

"We heard enough," Josh confirmed with a grin. "Now I can take my wife home and she won't be stewing about you and your lovelife all night."

"I knew you'd call her," Lily said with a sniff. She turned to her husband, who was only a couple of inches taller than she was, but built like a boxer, with dark good looks that were a nice contrast to

Lily's red hair and fair, freckled skin. "Let's go home and concentrate on *our* lovelife for a change, honey."

Josh swatted his wife on the fanny and gave her an affectionate leer. "Sounds like a plan to me."

Charles chuckled. "Get out of here, you two. You're embarrassing me."

"Your children are waiting for you in the kitchen, Charles," Lily called over her shoulder as Josh tugged her out the door and down the hall. "I frosted that cake Melissa made yesterday and they're chomping at the bit for their dessert. Better get in there before they climb the counter and help themselves."

"And our children are waiting for us in the minivan, Red, so we'd better get out there before they demolish the interior," Charles heard Josh warn his wife from somewhere in the living room.

Charles sauntered down the hall, too far behind them to catch up, and knowing they didn't expect or want him to, anyway. "Hey, thanks, you guys!" he yelled.

"It was our pleasure," Lily yelled back, then the front door slammed behind them.

Charles stopped in the hall, his hands in his pocket. He needed one more quiet, reflective moment before diving into the chaos of kids, chocolate cake, baths and bedtime stories. He was glad he'd decided to call Melissa, and would have done so even without Lily's encouragement.

Watching the interview on television had reminded him again how much he cared about her. It would be stupid to throw away a chance for happiness just because he was too angry, or too cautious, to listen to Melissa's explanation.

He was probably being paranoid about Brad, anyway. She'd said during the interview that her ex-husband wasn't going to be part of her baby's life, and that had to mean Brad wasn't going to be part of *her* life, either.

No. He shouldn't worry. Brad showing up today was probably just to get a glimpse of the baby, because he'd immediately disappeared after the interview…along with that cute, red-headed nurse. Yes, it looked like Brad had moved on.

Chapter Ten

Melissa couldn't help a startled laugh. "Brad, have you been drinking? You're not making any sense."

Brad pushed off from the closed door, his hands sunk deep into the pockets of a pair of khaki pants. He wore a white polo shirt that showed off his deep tan and made his blue eyes stand out even more strikingly. He took two slow steps toward the bed, then stopped and stared, his expression still as serious and intense as when he'd first arrived.

"Brad, you're giving me the creeps," Melissa finally said. "Say something. Explain why you're here. We had an agreement. A legal and binding agreement, I might add, that you were more than eager to sign. You have no rights concerning my baby. You gave me full custody—"

"Settle down, Missy," Brad said, pulling his hands free and lifting them, palms out, to make his point. "I know I don't have any rights...not legally, anyway."

"Not legally, and not in any other way, shape or form," Melissa answered tersely. "You never wanted me to have a baby, although you tricked me into thinking you did, then sabotaged my efforts to get pregnant by having sex with me only when you thought I wasn't fertile.'' Melissa raised a haughty brow. ''Turns out you didn't calculate well enough.''

''That's old news, isn't it, Missy?'' Brad said bitterly. Then, seeming to check himself, he snatched a furtive glance at her and continued in a conciliatory tone. ''Look, I know that was a mistake.''

''And not your only one, either. How does Rachel like California? Does she miss all her friends at the insurance company?'' Melissa hadn't been able to resist bringing up the name of the receptionist at Brad's last place of employment, whose taste for jewelry had made paying off the credit cards much harder.

Brad frowned. ''Rachel and I split two months ago. Besides, I never asked her to go to California with me. She followed me.''

''It doesn't matter,'' Melissa told him. ''I'd already decided to divorce you and had moved out before I knew anything at all about your affair with Rachel. She—and the others—were just an unpleasant surprise addition to the list of reasons why our marriage didn't work, Brad.''

''I don't believe that. I think Rachel *was* the reason our marriage broke up. I think you would have forgiven me for anything except being with another woman. And I only turned to her because you equated sex with getting pregnant, which took all the fun out of it.''

Melissa shrugged and said nothing. She wasn't going to be drawn into a nasty rehashing of the reasons why they'd split up. Everything Brad said just proved he'd never really known her, never understood what she really wanted from their marriage, and still didn't. And he was lying about the other women. She knew Rachel wasn't the only affair, just as Brad had to be stupid or crazy not to know that the marriage was a failure even before he started cheating. She just wished it hadn't taken *her* such a long time to figure that out.

Brad waited, then took another tentative step toward Melissa's bed. Her look warned him not to venture closer.

"Look, Melissa, just let me have my say, then I'll leave."

"You promise?" she asked drily.

"Absolutely."

She knew from past experiences that his promises were worthless, but she figured he wasn't going to leave till he was good and ready, or her father threw him out, so she just shrugged again. But the careless gesture was enough encouragement for Brad. He took a deep breath and began.

"As I said, I know I made mistakes with you, Melissa. I took you for granted. I cheated on you. You wanted a baby and I didn't, even though I pretended I was finally convinced otherwise. I didn't care what you wanted, and I admit I avoided lovemaking when I figured you were most likely to get pregnant."

"Old news, Brad," Melissa murmured, repeating his own earlier complaint. It *was* old news, but it was still painful to have it discussed again. And he was only saying what he thought she wanted to hear. Why was he doing this?

"But I've had time to think since I've been in California—"

"You mean you've had time to realize that I was

a darn good deal, right, Brad?'' Melissa interrupted, some of own bitterness spilling out against her will. ''I cleaned for you, cooked for you, slept with you, worked while you went to school and then kept working while you drifted from one job to another. It was easy to quit when you knew I was willing to support us both, wasn't it? And I was stupid and naive enough to think that all I had to do was be patient and keep on loving you and supporting you, and one day I'd get the family that I'd always craved. But you didn't care about what I wanted, Brad. You only cared about what *you* wanted. What's different now?''

''I care about what you want, Melissa,'' Brad insisted, his hands held wide. ''And I've realized that *I* want what you want, too. I want a family. I want to be a father to our baby.''

''It's too late, Brad. It doesn't matter what you want now. You're not going near my baby.'' Melissa wasn't falling for his contrite act. She'd seen it before. Maybe this was the best performance she'd seen to date, but he knew the odds were against him and the stakes were high, so he was laying it on thick.

''Can't I just see him?''

''You saw him when you watched the interview.''

''I was too far away. Does he look like me?''

Melissa glared at Brad, distrusting his plaintive look. She wished he'd leave. His act was so good, she almost believed that he was actually feeling some fatherly angst. But experience told her she'd be a fool to let him get to her.

She changed the subject. ''How did you even know I'd had the baby?''

''I was visiting my friend, Mel...you know the

guy I played football with at the U? Big blond guy? Played running back? He was at the house a lot. We watched tons of Monday-night football together.''

Melissa said nothing. How was she supposed to remember all those guys who over the years put their feet on her coffee table while she served them chips and beer?

"Anyway, he works in the maintenance department here at the hospital. Some coincidence, huh? I've been in Salt Lake since last Saturday, looking for a job. Mel's divorced, too, and he's letting me stay with him for a few days. He was standing right there when you came off the elevator.''

"Well, that mystery's solved,'' Melissa said, trying to disguise her alarm and disappointment that Brad was apparently planning to move back to Salt Lake City.

"I saw the interview just now on the television in the waiting room.'' Brad smiled the smile that used to make Melissa melt. "You looked great, Melissa.''

Her lack of response must have disconcerted him because the dazzling smile slipped a little, but he wasn't ready to give up. "You look even better in person. And...and I was really impressed with the way you've started that baby-food business, all on your own. I had no idea you wanted to do something like that.''

"Because you never listened to me,'' she said quietly. "It's been a dream of mine for a long time. A dream I mentioned more than once.''

Now the smile fell away completely. Brad knew he was striking out. He made one last desperate bid.

Tenderly, he said, "I still love you, Melissa. I want you back. Can't you at least give me a chance?''

Melissa shook her head, which was starting to ache from tension. "It's too late, Brad."

Brad's tender tone was gone when he demanded, "Why? Why is it too late, Melissa? Because of that damned Professor Avery?"

Tears were gathering in Melissa's eyes. She hated this. She hated that a devotion that had lasted over fourteen years was ending like this. If there was a slim chance that Brad truly still had feelings for her, she hated hurting him. Despite the pain he'd caused her, she had no taste for revenge.

"It wouldn't matter if I'd never met Charles," she told him truthfully. "I don't love you anymore, Brad."

Finally Brad was silenced. Melissa searched his face for a reaction. She thought she detected wounded pride...but not the heartfelt pain of loving someone who didn't love you back. She knew then that Brad wasn't there pleading his case because he still loved her. He was there because he wanted her back in his life for the same reasons he'd wanted her before. To take care of him.

But Melissa already had a baby. She didn't need another one. Especially not a baby who was thirty-two years old.

While Brad continued to stand there scowling, the door opened and Melissa's parents walked in. An anxious lump collected in her chest as she wondered what Brad would do. Pam was holding the baby and she froze like a statue. George's face turned red as a beet.

Brad watched the angry color flooding his ex-father-in-law's face and wisely decided to leave. But not before he bared his teeth in an unpleasant smile and said, "Nice to see you again, George. Pam. Good night." Then, correctly assuming he wouldn't get a similarly polite reply, he exited the room.

"Are you okay?" Pam asked, holding the baby against her shoulder as she searched Melissa's face for a clue as to what had gone on between her and Brad.

Melissa nodded, but was glad to be able to lean back into her pillows, close her eyes, and concentrate on releasing the pent up tension in her aching shoulders and neck.

"I'm okay," she said.

"What did he want?" George demanded.

Melissa gave a sad little laugh. "He says he wants me back. He says he wants to be a father to the baby and begged me to let him see his son."

"Brad didn't even glance at the baby!" Pam scoffed.

"He's so full of bull—"

"George...."

"He's full of it, as usual," George amended. "He's got some kind of agenda. Don't let him get to you, hon."

"Don't worry, Dad," Melissa assured him. "I have no illusions about his feelings for me. He just wants me back to make his life easier. And I know how I feel about *him,* so there's no danger there. I did wonder if he might actually have feelings for the baby. But as you said, Mom, he didn't even look at the baby, much less try to hold him."

"Do you think he'll be back?" Pam asked worriedly.

Melissa looked out the window as the long shadows of afternoon fell over the foothills. "I don't know, Mom."

TEN O'CLOCK Friday morning, the presents started arriving. Melissa was walking up and down the hallway, pushing her baby's crib ahead of her, when she saw two volunteers in melon-colored smocks navigating the first cartload past her. Both cheerful-looking ladies were in their later years, like Hester. Melissa raised her eyebrows at the huge haul of baby loot and wondered if one or two of those flower arrangements or teddy bears might be going to her room.

Once she'd finished her gentle exercising, Melissa returned to her room and stopped in the doorway, unable to believe her eyes! Vases of beautiful flowers bedecked every available surface. Boxes of disposable diapers and baby toiletries were placed in neat piles in the corners of the room. Teddy bears and squeaky toys, rattles and teething rings were scattered at the foot of her bed. Three baskets of fruit and a gigantic chocolate bar shaped like a binkie took up all the room on the tray table that swung over her bed.

One of the volunteers who was busily arranging this bounty, saw her standing there with her mouth open and exclaimed, "Oh, I *thought* it was you we passed in the hall! Ms. Richardson, it looks like lots of people saw your interview yesterday and you and the baby have some well-wishers!"

Melissa thought "some" well-wishers was an understatement. "I never expected anything like this to happen."

"This always happens with the first baby of the

New Year, but I think your story's actually more interesting. You have some mail, too.''

Melissa was perplexed. ''Mail? How could I have mail already?''

The volunteer reached into the bottom of her cart and starting pulling out express-mail envelopes and boxes. She piled them on the end of Melissa's bed, too. ''Where there's a will, there's a way.''

Melissa rolled her baby's crib to the side of her bed, made sure he was covered up against the hospital's air-conditioned climate, then sat down and started opening her mail. The volunteers hung around for a while, watching and marveling as Melissa pulled out large checks and money orders, cards and gift certificates to different baby-related businesses around town. One gift certificate, however, came from the Grand America Hotel downtown, good for a weekend in the honeymoon suite. The gift-giver had signed his name ''Anonymous'' and scrawled, ''For you and the professor.''

While Melissa blushed, the volunteers giggled and exclaimed and finally shuffled out of the room, pulling their empty cart behind them. Melissa was sure they'd be spreading the news about her many gifts all over the hospital…especially the romantic weekend at the Grand America. She shook her head ruefully, but didn't regret opening the gifts in front of such an appreciative audience. They took as much delight—actually more—in her good fortune as she did.

Volunteers continued to bring cartloads all day. By mid-afternoon, Melissa's family was transporting the gifts from the hospital to her apartment, averaging a trip every hour. The best gift, however, came by phone.

Melissa had been receiving phone calls all day and her brother, Craig, put himself in charge of weeding them out. Most were just good-hearted people that wanted to congratulate her or "chat," unaware that they might be among hundreds of callers keeping the baby up with the incessant ringing of the phone. Surprisingly, the baby slept through it all, only waking to eat.

"I'm going to have the operator refuse any more calls," Craig announced at five o'clock. "You'll never get any peace if this keeps up."

"Oh, let's let the calls come through for another hour or so," Melissa said, not wanting to miss it if Charles called her. She knew he was probably very busy with the children and trying to get his lecture fine-tuned for tomorrow, but there was always a *chance* he'd call.

Craig grinned at her knowingly.

At five-thirty, Craig took another phone call and Melissa's heart started beating faster as she watched his face light up. She couldn't imagine that he'd be as excited as she was that Charles called, but who else could it be?

"Sis," Craig whispered hoarsely, his hand over the speaking end of the phone receiver. "You're not going to believe this!"

Everyone else in the crowded room, family, volunteers, and healthcare providers, stopped talking and started listening, too. "Well, who…who is it, Craig?" Melissa stammered.

"It's some bigwig from Schuler's Baby Food

Company. I think they want to do business with you, Missy!''

Melissa's hands were shaking as she took the phone from Craig. Schuler's was the biggest baby-food company in the United States. In the whole *world!* What exactly did they want with her?

Five minutes later, Melissa knew what they wanted, and she was in shock. After hanging up the phone, she looked around at all the expectant faces in the room and said in a voice hoarse with emotion, ''They want to finance my baby-food line. In fact, they want to make Missy's Kid Cuisine a subsidiary of Schuler's! And they want me to be head of development!''

A general cheer went up, but Melissa's father needed facts before he could be unequivocally happy.

''How do they even know your stuff's good, Missy? *I* know it's good, but how do *they* know?''

''They flew someone in and had them buy a jar of every variety! Then they flew everything back to Houston, the headquarters of Schuler's, and did a bunch of testing and tasting.''

''Is that legal?'' George wondered aloud.

''As long as they don't steal my recipes,'' Melissa assured him. ''But, anyway, they loved my food! That was the President of Marketing and Research at Schuler's on the phone! They said they'd decided recently to launch a for-toddlers-only line, and since I'd already developed good-tasting, nutritionally sound recipes—not to mention, it's already got some pretty darn good advertising on the national news!—they wanted me to be part of the Schuler's family. Yeah, that's just how they said it! And they want to get on this right away, while my story's still fresh in the public's mind." Melissa beamed at all the astonished faces around her, feeling just as astonished as they looked. "Isn't this crazy and bizarre...and *wonderful?*"

"They're still going to call it Missy's Kid Cuisine, aren't they?" her father asked, still cautious.

"Yes, they're perfectly happy with the name. Mostly, I suppose, because that's what was touted on TV."

"Makes sense. But get it in writing, Missy. Get it all in writing. Do you have a lawyer? You know, besides the one who helped you with the divorce?"

Melissa smiled. "No, but I'm sure you can refer me to yours, Dad. Don't worry, I'll make sure it's all done right. They're calling me back on Monday so we can set a date to meet and go over the details."

Satisfied that they'd heard all there was to hear, the volunteers and nurses in the room hurried out the door and started spreading the news. Melissa knew that soon everyone in the hospital would know. She felt a niggling of unease as she recalled that Brad's friend worked in the hospital, and that he would undoubtedly pass on the information to Brad. But what difference would that make? Brad would probably wish he could cash in on Melissa's good fortune, but he wouldn't be able to. They were divorced and had no ties whatsoever. Not even through the baby... legally speaking.

Melissa firmly put Brad out of her mind. She was too happy to let him spoil this moment, this day, for her. She was so happy she wanted to hug herself...or better yet, hug someone else. Like Charles, maybe? She was dying to tell him the news, but didn't dare call and disturb him. She'd kept him away from his paper all week and now he had only one day left before the big lecture. She'd have to hold on to her news—and her hug—till Saturday.

CHARLES HAD CONCLUDED his lecture at Kingsbury Hall on the University of Utah campus and was trying to exit the building, but people just weren't letting him go. For a Saturday, and just the second day in a row that Salt Lake City was enjoying temperatures that reached only to the mid-nineties, you'd think his esteemed colleagues, representing various fields of science, would have something better to do than question and tease him about his appearance on television!

Charles was being polite and good-natured about it, but enough was enough. And where were the questions he usually got after one of his lectures? You know, questions that actually pertained to the lecture?

"I have an appointment and I'm going to be late if I don't leave immediately," Charles finally announced.

"Wait, Professor Avery," came a frustrated voice from the back of the crowd. "I have a question about your lecture. Your theory about Ursa Major intrigues me…and I was wondering how close you were to getting a patent on your new telescope lens?"

A young man, obviously an eager astronomy student or buff, squeezed his way through the crowd. Charles glanced at his watch. It was 1:45. He'd told Melissa that he'd be at her apartment by two.

"Walk with me and we'll talk on the way to my car," he told the short, plump, slightly disheveled young man, who eagerly fell in step beside him. Charles waved and smiled at everyone else and they reluctantly let him go. Charles shook his head, astounded by all the attention he was getting because of the television interview. He could only imagine what had been happening to Melissa over the past two days. He'd wanted to call her, had thought about her constantly since their last, brief telephone conversation on Wednesday night, but he'd forced himself to wait. They'd both needed the time apart. Time to think. Time to get their bearings. Time for her to spend with her baby and family. Time for him to finish his lecture—

Suddenly Charles remembered his walking companion, huffing and puffing and straining to keep up with his long, impatient strides across the parking lot.

Charles slowed down. "I'm sorry. I'm a little preoccupied. And I'm in a bit of a hurry, so what's your first question?"

"Is Melissa Richardson's baby really yours, Professor Avery?" the breathless young man inquired, thrusting a small tape recorder under Charles's nose.

Charles stopped in his tracks, frowning. "What kind of question is that? And who the hell are you? I thought you wanted to ask me questions about my lecture."

The young man smiled sheepishly. "I know all I want to know about celestial bodies, Professor Avery. At least the ones up there." He jabbed his finger heavenward. "I'm more interested in you and Melissa Richardson. As a reporter from the *National Intruder*, I'm prepared to pay you top dollar for an exclusive interview."

"I've already given an interview," Charles said,

angry that he'd been tricked, but all too aware that if he made a scene the reporter would make a story out of it...especially since he had no intention of providing him with the "exclusive" interview he wanted. "If you watched the news Wednesday night, you already know everything there is to know."

"But I don't buy that, Professor—"

Charles started walking, this time glad he was so easily able to outstrip the out-of-shape reporter who was trying to walk and talk at the same time. Charles finally reached his car and got in. He slammed the door shut, started the ignition and put the car in gear. The reporter finally caught up with him, firing questions and offering money while he stood directly in front of Charles's SUV.

Now Charles was really getting ticked off. He allowed the vehicle to roll forward slightly, hoping the man would think he was actually capable of running him down. The bumper butted up against the man's thighs, but, although he glanced down nervously, he continued to plead his case. Another slight roll forward and Charles's grim look must have convinced the man that he was seriously angry, if not actually a cold-blooded killer, and he stepped out of the way.

Charles breathed a sigh of relief as he drove the car out of the parking lot, headed for Sugarhouse and Melissa. He couldn't believe what was happening! It angered and repulsed him to think that a tabloid magazine wanted to make something scandalous out of Melissa's story. It was lucky she and the baby had even survived such an unusual birth, and that and Melissa's courage was the *real* story here, not some trumped-up romance between a man and his nanny, á la *Jane Eyre*. Hell, there was *nothing* going on between him and Melissa.

Well, that wasn't exactly true, either, Charles admitted to himself. There was something going on between them, only he wasn't sure what. And it was nobody's business but theirs.

Charles was a private person by nature. He'd only given the interview for Melissa's sake, hoping the publicity for Missy's Kid Cuisine would pay off and help make Melissa an independent woman. He'd do it again...for Melissa. But not for any other reason he could possibly imagine.

Charles tried to relax, but in addition to the irritation of ditching the tabloid reporter, he was worried about the upcoming conversation with Melissa. Sure, he wanted to see her, he'd missed her and knew he cared about her, but they still had to clear the air about why she'd lied to him about Brad. He wanted to understand and accept her explanation and was more than willing to forgive. But even if he immediately and completely understood why she'd lied, he still had an uneasy feeling about Brad....

Were she and Brad *really* finished? If so, why had he shown up at the hospital? And even if Melissa sincerely believed they were finished, could Brad change her mind? He'd been her whole life in high school, had fooled and finagled her for years. Especially now that they shared a son...could Brad still get to her?

MELISSA BADE GOODBYE to her parents at noon, assuring them that she and the baby would be fine and that they could check on her later in the day...after she and Charles had had time alone together to talk.

Her parents were just as eager for Melissa to clear things up with Charles, but they left her reluctantly. They said they weren't sure she was physically rested enough to handle the baby on her own, but Melissa suspected they were mostly concerned that Brad might harass her...especially now that she was about to sign a lucrative business deal.

Melissa had to admit she was a little worried about that, too. If Brad thought she was going to be making a lot of money —which she was if Schuler's came through on their initial salary promises—he probably wouldn't be able to resist trying one more time to win her back.

But Brad didn't have her address, and the hospital had been specifically cautioned—particularly in light of the fact that she'd become a bit of a celebrity— to keep her personal information inaccessible to everyone except the business office, for billing and insurance purposes. Brad's friend, Mel, worked in maintenance at the hospital, so he would not be authorized to access her files. Her home phone was unpublished, too, so Brad wouldn't be able to find her address in the telephone directory. She felt she was safe from a visit from Brad for a while, anyway, if not forever. And when and if he did show up, although it would be an unpleasant chore, Melissa knew she could handle him.

Today she expected one visitor. Charles. And she could hardly wait!

The baby was asleep in his crib, but the house was in chaos. There were presents piled everywhere that needed to be organized and put away—some of it given away to women's shelters and friends, considering how much she'd received—but first things first! She wanted to look pretty for Charles.

Pam had brought a maternity blouse and pants to the hospital for Melissa to wear home, but Melissa was delighted to note how loosely they fit her. She knew she had to expect a bit of a tummy for a few more days, but she'd immediately noticed a drop in water retention right after the baby was born. Her hands and, best of all, her ankles were no longer swollen!

Melissa rummaged through her closet, eyed her jeans but was afraid she'd be mortified and discouraged if she tried to get those on three days after giving birth, then finally settled on a pale yellow sundress she'd worn last summer that skimmed her figure without hugging it, and showed off her legs and once-again-trim ankles.

She showered quickly—listening for the baby with the door open the whole time—fixed her hair and makeup, put on her dress and felt so refreshed and renewed, her confidence got a nice shot in the arm. She needed that shot in the arm, too, because she had much more to worry about than looking pretty for Charles. She had to explain to him why she'd lied about Brad and hope he'd understand. She didn't want to lose him because of her own stupid pride.

Precisely at 1:55 the doorbell rang. Excited to see Charles, but oh-so-nervous, too, she took a deep breath and walked with measured steps to the door.

Melissa smiled brightly…but the smile fell away the minute she opened the door.

Instead of Charles on her doorstep, there stood Brad.

Chapter Eleven

Worse than the fact that Brad had found out her address so quickly and easily, or even that she was having to deal with him so much sooner than she anticipated, was the fact that his timing was terrible! Charles was going to be there any minute!

Or was his timing...*perfect?*

Melissa eyed her ex-husband with suspicion and distaste. It wasn't that he didn't look good. He looked great. The navy-blue knit shirt he was wearing fit his torso snugly, revealing the fact that he'd lost the gut he'd developed from watching too much television and consuming too much beer and barbecued hotwings over the years.

"Hello, Missy," Brad said, smiling innocently around a huge bouquet of yellow roses...her favorite flower. His gaze traversed the length of her, lingering on her breasts, which were fuller than usual because she was nursing. "Wow, you look great. I thought pregnancy might ruin that gorgeous figure of yours, but looks like I was wrong."

"Brad, why are you here? And why are you here *now?*"

He continued with the innocent act. "What's wrong with now? Are you expecting somebody?"

"You know I am. You were eavesdropping when I was talking to Charles on the phone Wednesday night. You overheard me tell him to meet me here today. At two o'clock. And that's how you knew where I lived, too. Right?"

Brad shrugged. "I wasn't eavesdropping. I just happened to be right outside the door when I heard you talking on the phone. I peeked in and you looked so—" He paused, sneered slightly, then continued. "—*blissed out,* I decided to wait till you were through with the conversation before I intruded. I accidentally heard you telling your professor when and where to meet you today."

"But you had no qualms about intruding today, did you? You're here now because I'm expecting Charles."

Brad's chin jutted out ever so slightly. "All's fair in love and war, Missy."

"This is not about love, Brad," Melissa argued. "You aren't in love with me. You're here because you think I can be useful to you. Especially now that I'm about to sign a contract with Schuler's and would probably be able to support you in the lifestyle you've always thought you deserved."

"Missy, I did hear about the phone call from Schuler's," Brad admitted in that same sincere, ingenuous tone. "That's partly why I'm here, just to congratulate you. I'm so proud of you, kid!" He reached out and caressed Melissa's upper arm. She flinched and pulled away.

"I'm not buying this act, Brad," she insisted. "Now, I want you to go...before Charles gets here."

Brad didn't move. He studied her face, probably trying to come up with some other excuse for sticking around, some new and better story that Melissa might believe.

Finally he sighed, the bouquet of roses flopping against his thigh as his arm went lax. "I don't know what to do to convince you I'm really in love with you, Missy. And that I've changed. Maybe someday… But today's not the day, I guess."

Melissa waited and watched, her heart full of misgiving and distrust. She couldn't believe he was giving up so easily, or so graciously.

"Can I just see the baby once before I go?"

That question was unexpected and most unwelcome. If Brad had any ability to influence her feelings, to make her feel guilt or sympathy or fear or any emotion at all, it was through the baby. She felt so much love for her newborn son, she couldn't imagine Brad being a father to the same precious child and not wanting to see him and hold him. And denying him a glimpse of his child before he went away again for good, seemed cruel. But did she dare?

"Look, I know you don't have to let me see him," Brad said. "But I'm just asking you, as his father, to give me a little slack here. I won't touch him if you don't want me to. And then, after I've seen him, I'll leave. I promise."

Melissa chewed on her bottom lip. Brad's habitual smugness was nowhere in sight. She'd never seen him so humble or so apparently sincere. Was it possible he truly did have some genuine paternal feelings toward the child they'd created together?

Any minute Charles would be arriving…but it would only take a minute to show Brad the baby.

Then he'd leave. He wouldn't have another single excuse to stay. And, if she was quick and lucky, she could get rid of him before Charles showed up.

"All right," she said. "But stay right where you are. I'll bring the baby to you. You can see him, but that's all. You might be the biological father, Brad, but you signed away any rights you had to be his real father."

Brad's expression remained humble. "I know that, Missy. You don't have to keep reminding me."

Melissa felt a spasm of guilt. How did he manage to make her feel even the tiniest bit guilty? she wondered, as she went quickly into the bedroom to get the baby out of his crib. Brad hadn't wanted to be a father to their baby, and he definitely didn't deserve her sympathy, but she couldn't seem to help herself.

The baby was fast asleep and she hated disturbing him. But she wanted to get rid of Brad and couldn't wait till the baby woke up on his own. She picked him up and he startled awake, then immediately began crying.

"I'm sorry, sweetheart," she crooned, bouncing him gently. "I was hoping I wouldn't wake you."

"He does look like me, doesn't he?"

Now it was Melissa's turn to be startled. "I told you to stay where you were, Brad! I don't want you in my house, much less my bedroom."

"I heard him crying," Brad protested, reaching across her to take the baby's flailing fist in his hand. The baby latched on to Brad's finger. "Hey, the kid's got a great grip. Won't have any trouble holding a baseball bat."

"All babies have strong grips," Melissa told him

repressively. "He only grabbed on to you because it's instinctive."

"Let me hold him, Melissa."

"No, Brad, I told you—"

But Brad wasn't going to take no for an answer. Short of causing harm to her child, there was no way Melissa could prevent Brad from taking him out of her arms.

Inside, Melissa was seething, too angry to speak. She was sick and frightened and felt she'd totally lost control of the situation. *How had he managed this?*

But it didn't matter how he'd managed it. She obviously still couldn't keep Brad from bullying her. She resolved then and there that the minute Brad was gone, she was going to make a call to her lawyer and get a restraining order to keep him away from her and her baby.

Not that he was ever physically abusive. But he'd been emotionally abusive and she wasn't going to let him insinuate himself into her baby's life and possibly damage him emotionally, too.

Brad obviously had no clue how to hold the baby, so Melissa stood very close and supported the baby's fragile head and neck in the cup of her hand.

"Maybe he'll be a baseball player, instead of a football player, like his dad," Brad was saying as he smiled down at the baby. "But it doesn't matter which sport he chooses, or sports, for that matter. I'm sure he'll be good at everything. Yep, just like his ol' dad."

Melissa said nothing. Her vision was blurring. She was fighting back angry, helpless tears. She just wanted her baby back! She just wanted Brad to leave, and to leave her and the baby alone!

That's when she heard a sound at the door to the bedroom. A soft swishing sound, like someone's clothes brushing against the wall. She looked up and saw Charles, his hand on the knob of the bedroom door, his shoulder braced against the doorjamb.

Their gazes met and Melissa felt as though her heart was free-falling off a ten-story building. His expression was a mixture of incredulity, profound disappointment and a painful acknowledgment of betrayal.

Brad turned, too, and saw Charles standing there. But, for once, he said nothing. He didn't have to. He'd set the stage and the targeted audience of one had arrived precisely on cue.

"Charles," Melissa said, her throat so constricted her words came out in a tortured whisper. "Brad was just leaving. He—"

"No, I think I should be the one to go," Charles said quietly, his eyes averted now. "It looks like I interrupted a very tender scene." He turned and, with his back to them, said, "Goodbye, Melissa."

Charles walked down the carpeted hallway and out the front door...closing it behind him.

Melissa turned to Brad. "You left the front door open on purpose." It was a statement, not a question or even an accusation. Everything that had transpired had been Brad's plan all along. "You followed me in here, knew Charles would wonder why the front door was left standing wide open, then come in to see if everything was okay...only to find *you* holding the baby."

Again Brad kept silent, but Melissa detected the old smugness showing through the innocent facade. Brad was proud of the problems and unhappiness he'd just caused her.

"Give me my baby," she ordered, her voice steely with cold fury and resolve. "Give him to me now or I'll call the police."

Brad observed her briefly, then handed her the baby.

She hugged her baby close to her chest and pointed a trembling finger at the door. "Now leave."

Brad hesitated. He wasn't the sort of man that liked being told what to do, especially by a woman. But Melissa must have looked too tough to tangle with tonight. He turned on his heel and walked to the door, then turned back. "This isn't over, Missy," he promised her. Then he continued through the living room, opened the front door and was finally gone.

Melissa stood in the bedroom, rocking her baby until he settled back to sleep again. She laid him gently in his crib, then walked into the living room, latched the chain lock on the front door, moved to the sofa and plopped down against the cushions.

She stared at the door for a moment or two, then dropped her head into her hands and burst into tears.

Ten minutes later, she got control of herself and called her lawyer. Brad had threatened that things weren't over between them. He was wrong. He was never going to bully her, or trick her or make her feel sorry for him, ever again.

She may have lost any chance of having a future with Charles, but she wasn't going to let her future and her baby's future be ruined by her past.

Seven weeks later

IT WAS NEARLY two months ago and Charles still couldn't quite get out of his head that touching scene of a mother and father fondly gazing at their infant child.

Brad and Melissa had been standing close together... *intimately* close. He'd been holding the baby, smiling down at him, referring to himself as "dad." She'd been supporting the baby's head, her own head bent, her silky golden hair falling against Brad's chest.

Then she'd suddenly realized someone was in the room and looked up at Charles, her eyes glistening with emotion....

Had she forgotten that she'd invited him over so they could talk? So she could explain why she'd lied about Brad being dead? Or did she just deem the whole explanation a moot point, since it was obvious she'd let Brad back into her home and heart, even though she'd told him Brad was out of her life and the baby's life forever?

But he was adjusting. For the past few weeks Charles had kept feverishly busy. The hardest part had been trying to explain to the children why they couldn't see Melissa or the baby. But they were starting to forget, as children do, and that was certainly a blessing.

"Are we going to the fair, Dad?"

Charles had been sitting at his desk in the study for a couple of hours, but the tall stack of student reports he'd intended to read and grade had barely gone down. As so often happened lately, if he allowed himself to sit still too long, his mind went back to that whirlwind week Melissa had spent with them. He still missed her. It was crazy, he knew. It was stupid and pointless, but his heart seemed to have a mind of its own.

He hadn't heard a word from her since he'd interrupted the two of them with their child—the baby Charles had often wished was his—so he assumed that she and Brad had reconciled and—

"Dad! *Dad!*"

Charles turned to Christopher, who was trying to gain his attention not only by yelling in his ear, but by pounding Charles's knee with his small, but surprisingly hard, fist.

"Whoa, Christopher! I heard you. You can stop beating me now."

"Boy, Dad, sometimes you're off in your own little world."

Charles laughed. "I see you've picked up another of Mrs. Butters's little platitudes."

Christopher cocked his head to the side. "What's a platitude, Dad? Is it like a platypus?"

"No, it's another animal altogether."

"Do they have one at Hogle Zoo?"

Charles tried returning to the original question. "You wanted to know if we're going to the fair, right?"

This time Charles's diversion worked. Christopher smiled and nodded his head vigorously. "Yeah. Are we?"

Charles stood up, stretching the kinks out of his legs from sitting and thinking too long. Too bad he couldn't stretch the kinks out of his brain. "Of course we're going to the fair. Just as soon as your Aunt Lily and Uncle Josh get over here with your cousins."

Christopher did a little happy dance and clapped

his hands. "I can't wait! I'm going to ride the Scrambler and I'm going to see the baby pigs and I'm going to eat cotton candy and I'm going to see the Indians dance on the stage and—"

"Wow, did we manage to do all that last year?" Charles asked as he preceded his excited son out of the study.

"Yep, and we're going to do even *more* this year," Christopher predicted gleefully.

Charles chuckled to himself. Mrs. Butters was going with them, but it would take the combined and concerted effort of all four adults to handle six small children at the fair. Charles had a "leash" for Daniel, one of those made for keeping toddlers from running away and getting lost in public places. Lily and Josh would put the twins in the double-stroller and hold Amanda's hand. He and Mrs. Butters should be able to keep track of his three. By tonight they'd all be exhausted, but that's the way Charles liked going to bed these days…completely exhausted. It was the best way to guarantee sleep without too much thinking beforehand.

Josh and Lily showed up right after lunch and they set off for the Salt Lake County Fair in two vehicles. It was a beautiful mid-September day, the mild temperatures just right for strolling around a fair…or chasing around after six excited children. Mrs. Butters had dressed Christopher, Sarah, Daniel and even herself in bright red T-shirts and jeans. She figured the kids would be easier to spot in a crowd if they somehow got away from her.

Charles thought ruefully that Mrs. Butters would be hard to miss, too, which he was sure was entirely her intention. In addition to the fire-engine-red shirt, she tipped the scales at two hundred pounds and was five feet nine inches tall, with a beehive hairdo left-over from her teen days in the 1960s. The children couldn't stay lost for long with such a bright beacon guiding them back to safety.

They began with the Scrambler, since Christopher wouldn't be happy till he'd made himself dizzy, then proceeded to the stalls to look at farm animals.

At four o'clock, Lily announced, "I need some energy. Let's have some ice cream. I hear they're giving away free cones in the Products Exhibition Hall."

"A sample won't fill these kids up," Mrs. Butters warned, holding tight to the hands of Christopher and Sarah while they bounced and twirled off the ends of her fingers like a couple of yo-yos. "And the sugar might make them more hyper."

Charles thought Mrs. Butters had a point. But Lily insisted. "An article in the paper I read said it was a new kind of ice cream, made with a sugar substitute."

"Oh, yummy," Josh said with good-natured sarcasm.

Lily laughed. "Come on, let's try it. Besides, the article mentioned some other exhibits I'd like to see, too. We can walk through the hall, then when we come out on the other side, go directly to the food vendors for ice cream, or corn on the cob, or hotdogs, or whatever you guys want."

This sounded like a reasonable plan to Charles, and to everyone else who was paying attention—meaning none of the children—and they proceeded to the Products Exhibition Hall.

"Why are we goin' in here?" Sarah demanded to

know as they walked through the open door and into the barn-like building.

"Yeah," chorused her cousin, Amanda, also three and a half. "There's nothin' in here but *stuff*. It's like a gross'ry store!"

"Oh, but there's lots of neat stuff in here," Lily said, using her most enthusiastic and persuasive voice. "There's ice cream and there's—"

"There's M'lissa!" exclaimed Daniel, straining at the end of his leash and pointing a stubby little finger.

Charles looked in the direction toward which his small son pointed. Daniel was right. There was Melissa, surrounded by people and tables that were covered with jars and samples of her kid cuisine. Dressed in a tailored navy-blue pant suit, looking slim, shapely and professional, she had her baby strapped to her back papoose-style and was talking animatedly to the attentive audience.

Charles had thought he'd made progress over the past seven weeks. He was wrong. Seeing her again, he knew he was hopelessly in love with her.

Charles looked around and caught Lily's eye. Her chagrined, but unrepentant smile proved she'd known Melissa would be here. And with the children along, there was no way he could just turn around and walk away. A face-to-face encounter was inevitable. But what did Lily think she was accomplishing? If Melissa was with Brad, what was the point of seeing her again?

"Melissa!" Christopher exclaimed, pulling free from Mrs. Butters's hand and running toward the Missy's Kid Cuisine exhibit. Sarah tried to follow, but only managed to drag Mrs. Butters along at a slightly faster speed than normal. Daniel was stretching his leash to the point of snapping it in two, leading Charles inexorably closer and closer to the woman he loved…but couldn't have.

Charles gave Lily another stern look, but she only smiled, as if to say, "What's a sister for?"

MELISSA WAS JUST finishing up another scripted presentation and was looking forward to a break. The baby needed to eat and she needed to sit down for fifteen minutes. Her helpers, Brenda and Sheila, would take over while she took a breather.

"And now you're all invited, children *and* parents, to taste the many varieties you see on the table in front of you. There's plenty to go around and lots of plastic spoons and napkins in containers at the end of each table. Help yourself…and enjoy Missy's Kid Cuisine. My associates will be happy to answer any questions, and I'll be back in a few minutes if you want to talk to me. Thank you."

There was a smattering of applause and Melissa quickly turned and walked to the back of the raised platform. She stepped off and was about to head to the break room that had been set aside for the exhibitors, when a crowd of people literally surrounded her.

She was about to explain that she'd be happy to talk to them when she came back in fifteen minutes after feeding her baby, but then recognized that this was no ordinary crowd.

It was the *Avery* crowd…plus Lily and her brood, spouse included. Surprised and nearly trembling with nervous excitement, Melissa scanned the crowd— taking in all the sweet, remembered faces of the children she'd missed so desperately over the past two months—then settled her hungry gaze on Charles's face, the face she'd missed most of all.

He looked back at her, his expression a mixture of uncertainty, curiosity and a firmly-kept-in-check, tentative...joy. She knew just how he felt. Did she dare show how happy she was to see him, too? Or was she already doing that?

They both opened their mouths to say something, but Daniel beat them to it.

"M'lissa!" he crowed, flinging his arms around her legs. Christopher and Sarah both followed Daniel's example and nearly toppled her over.

"Whoa, kids!" Charles said, grabbing Melissa's elbow to steady her against the onslaught of affection.

Startled and touched, Melissa tousled their heads and bent—as far as she was able to with the baby on her back—to give them hugs. Daniel and Sarah babbled and smiled up at her, seeming to try to tell her everything that had happened in their lives—including seeing the baby pigs just an hour ago—since she'd last seen them. She couldn't believe they still felt so connected to her and her heart swelled with pleasure and gratitude!

"Wow, it's good to see you guys! I've missed you!"

"Then why didn't you come to see us?" Christopher asked her, apparently still as matter-of-fact and inquisitive as ever. He'd been more reserved than the other children, perhaps holding back because he was a little angry with her for staying away, and not knowing, either, if he'd see her again after today.

Melissa flitted an embarrassed glance toward

Charles, who immediately looked elsewhere. "I... I've been really busy, Christopher, what with the baby and the business and—"

"New mothers haven't got time to comb their hair, much less make social calls," Lily said, jumping in to save Melissa from further explanation.

Melissa smiled gratefully at her. "It's good to see you again, Lily. This must be your hubby?"

"Yeah, well, I can't get my boyfriend to do anything with the kids, so I had to bring Josh. Josh, this is Melissa Richardson."

Josh smiled, stepped forward and took Melissa's hand in a firm shake. "I recognize you from the television interview." He gestured toward the Missy's Kid Cuisine display. "Looks like the exposure did good things for your company. I read in the *Tribune* that you and Schuler's struck a deal."

Melissa nodded, darted another quick glance at Charles. "Yes. It's a wonderful opportunity, and I owe it all to the interview." This time she looked directly at Charles, held her gaze and compelled him to look back. "I'm so glad you convinced me to go through with it, Charles. And for sticking around yourself. I hope you haven't been hassled by the media in any way? I've had a few run-ins with tabloid reporters."

He returned her gaze for a moment, then looked away again. "Only once. Some guy from the *Intruder* waylaid me on my way to your house after that lecture in July. That's why I was a little late."

But not too late for Brad's plan, Melissa thought despairingly. She wanted to further explain about that day, to tell him that although it had taken more time and hassle than she'd expected, she'd made sure

Brad could never legally come within one hundred yards of her person, child or home again, but it wouldn't be appropriate to blurt out everything in front of his family and in such a public place. And maybe he didn't care anymore, anyway.

"This is Mrs. Butters," Charles said abruptly, drawing forth a middle-aged woman who had been standing slightly behind him.

"Mrs. Butters!" exclaimed Melissa, truly delighted to meet her. "I've heard so much about you. The children adore you."

Mrs. Butters smiled, but raised a rueful brow. "I could say the exact same things about you, Melissa. After I returned from New Orleans, it took me the better part of three weeks to make the children understand that we couldn't use *two* nannies on the premises."

"I told you, she doesn't have to be a *nanny*," Christopher scoffed. "She could be our m—"

"So, this is the little elevator angel," Mrs. Butters interrupted, peeking around Melissa's shoulder at the baby as she simultaneously grabbed Christopher loosely by the neck, then wrapped her arms around his chest and held him tight against her. Melissa thought that if she'd had some duct tape, Mrs. Butters might have been tempted to use that to keep Christopher mum! "Is he a good baby? He's certainly behaving like an angel right now!"

Despite her intense embarrassment at Christopher nearly saying the M-word, Melissa answered cheerfully. "He's a very good baby, but he's probably getting pretty hungry, which means if I don't feed him soon, he'll make a fuss and you'll decide he's not an angel at all.'' As if on cue, the baby started squirming and whimpering.

"We'd better go,'' Charles said, and Melissa couldn't help but notice and be deflated by the resolve in his voice. She wondered if it would make any difference if he knew she and Brad weren't— and hadn't been since before the divorce—an item? She's sure that was the impression he'd got when he'd come by that fatal Saturday in July.

"Well, I, for one, am not leaving before I see the baby,'' Lily announced.

Sarah and Amanda jumped up and down. "Yeah, we want t'see the baby!'' they chanted together.

Daniel had wrapped his leash twice around Charles while skipping in circles during the boring adult conversations, but now he was all attention. "Where's the baby?'' he demanded. "I don't see 'im.''

"He's on my back,'' Melissa said with a smile. "And if one of you will extract him from my baby backpack, I'll be happy to show him off.'' She turned her back to them, wondering who would step forward and pluck the baby out of his carrier.

Charles figured there was a conspiracy going on. When all of the acknowledged baby-lovers in the family suddenly turned shy, he had no choice but to hand over Daniel's leash to Josh and take the baby out of the carrier himself. He was forced to stand close enough to Melissa to smell her hair and her faint, alluring perfume, which was wonderfully spicy and faintly oriental.

The baby smelled good, too, as he lifted him out of the carrier and settled him into the crook of his arm...all powdery and new and clean. Charles couldn't help but smile down at him…after all, he was Melissa's. Not to mention he was such a handsome little guy. The dark, dark hair he'd been born with had softened to a downy light brown. His vivid blue eyes, spiked with long, dark lashes, stared up at Charles, as if to say, "Who the heck are you?" But he must have liked Charles because suddenly he smiled back, his whole face transformed into a vision of boyish charm.

Charles couldn't help a delighted chuckle and, for the first time, an unselfconscious exchange of smiles with Melissa. "Oh, he's a great kid, Missy."

"Let us see, too, Dad," Christopher complained, tugging on Charles's pants pocket. Charles squatted and held his armful of beautiful baby for the children to see. They gathered around, seemingly awestruck, staring and not even squirming for once.

After a minute or two of this strangely quiet contemplation, Christopher looked up at Melissa and asked, "What's his name, Melissa?"

Charles looked at her, too. They all looked at her…and waited. They waited while she blushed the deepest shade of rose Charles had ever seen on another human being.

Lily laughed. "Why are you blushing, Melissa? You *have* named him, haven't you?"

Melissa nodded. "Yes. I've named him."

"So, what's his name?" Christopher demanded.

Melissa took in a huge breath, then let it out slowly before announcing, "His name is…Avery."

Chapter Twelve

Charles was stunned and speechless. Fortunately, or unfortunately, depending on how you looked at it, Christopher was not similarly handicapped.

"*Avery?* But that's a last name, isn't it? That's *our* last name." Using his fingers to keep track, he started counting and naming each member of the family. "Christopher Dale Avery. Sarah Jane Avery. Daniel Winston—"

"We get the picture, Christopher," Lily broke in as she shot Charles a meaningful look.

"Murphy Brown named her sitcom kid Avery, didn't she?" Josh said.

"I don't think that's why Melissa named *her* baby Avery," Lily hissed in Josh's ear. "But maybe if we took the kids to get that ice cream, Melissa and Charles could talk and—"

Charles stood up, still holding the baby…or rather, *Avery.*

"What does Brad think of the name?" he asked, getting right down to the nitty-gritty. He'd been watching Melissa since she'd revealed Avery's name. The blush on her cheeks was still blazing away, and she hadn't been able to look him in the eye since Christopher had asked the seemingly innocent question.

While everyone remained silent, Melissa appeared to be composing herself, or drumming up courage. Charles waited, holding his breath. He couldn't get over it.... *She'd named her son Avery!* What exactly did that mean?

Eventually, Melissa looked at Charles and held his gaze unblinkingly. With a little quiver in her voice at first, then more firmly, she said, "Brad had nothing to do with choosing Avery's name. Brad is not Avery's father. He will never be his father, legally or otherwise. I haven't seen Brad since that day in July when you found him holding Avery. And what you saw was not what it—"

"But I thought Brad was dead," Christopher interrupted, his brow furrowed. He turned to Charles. "Dad, *you* said Melissa's husband was dead."

There was a collective cringe among the adults and the tension in the air was thick enough to choke on. Charles hadn't gotten around to clearing up that little untruth he'd mistakenly told his son about Brad being dead. He hadn't expected to find the need to do so, since he'd thought Melissa was lost from their lives forever.

"I know that's what I said, Christopher," Charles began. "But I was wrong."

Christopher's eyes grew large. "You mean he's alive? Geez, Dad, how could you think someone was dead when he really wasn't?"

"I'll explain it to you later at home," Charles promised him. "But right now I'd like to talk with Melissa, so—"

Charles felt Melissa's hand on his arm, drawing

him slightly away from the others. He looked down into her blue eyes, which were full of apology. "I'm sorry I put you in this spot. Why don't I just take Avery to the break room and feed him, and you and your family can go back to having a fun day at the fair?" She sighed and smiled sadly. "I've caused you so much trouble, Charles. But I really didn't mean to. I'm so sorry."

She held out her arms for Avery and Charles automatically handed him over, all the while searching Melissa's face, trying to understand exactly what was going on in her head. Better yet, it would definitely promote better understanding if he knew exactly what was going on in her *life*.

Before she could walk away, he said, "Look, Melissa, this isn't a good time or place to talk. But I got the impression you weren't through telling me everything you wanted to about that day in July when I found you and Brad together with the baby."

She shrugged, fussed with the baby's clothes, did everything but look at him. "No. But maybe I don't have the right to ask you to listen to any more explanations."

Despite the seriousness of the situation, Charles chuckled. "Any more explanations? Hell, Melissa, I don't think I've heard even one explanation all the way through before getting interrupted by someone or something. If you think there's a chance we could have an uninterrupted hour to talk sometime, I'll come by your apartment."

Suddenly Melissa looked up, her eyes misty with emotion, a smile trembling on her lips. "With a two-month-old in the house, I can't promise we won't be interrupted, but I can promise that he's the only one you'll have to worry about.''

Charles liked the sound of that.

''When?''

''Well…how about tonight?''

''What time?''

''Eight-thirty? But, listen, I bought a house and this is my new address—''

FOUR HOURS LATER, Charles was on his way to Melissa's new residence just a few blocks away from her old apartment. It was just past sundown and the air was still warm from the September sunshine they'd enjoyed all day long. He'd showered and shaved and was wearing a sage-green polo shirt and jeans. He'd thought about dressing up a bit, but this wasn't a date and he didn't want to come on too strong. It was enough that they were finally going to be able to have a private, honest conversation!

He just hoped he could handle the honest truth. There was still a lot he didn't understand. He'd had a hell of a time trying to explain to Christopher why he'd thought Brad was dead, and ended up telling him—in simple terms—that he'd heard it from a ''credible source'' who had proven to be wrong. For some reason, Charles didn't want to bring up Melissa during the difficult discussion, didn't want Christopher disillusioned about her. Besides, if Melissa's explanation satisfied Charles, what was the point of telling Christopher where the ''highly exaggerated rumors'' about Brad's death had originated?

The address Melissa had given him took him to a quiet residential street in an old, upscale neighborhood of Sugarhouse. The houses were mid-century, but well-kept and charming, the streets lined with trees. It would be a good place to bring up a child, which was probably what Melissa had had in mind when she'd bought the place.

Charles parked in front of the white stucco bungalow and went to the solid-oak front door, the top of which was curved in the cottage style. With butterflies in his stomach, he knocked on the door and looked nervously around the small, tidily landscaped yard, illuminated partly by the porch light and partly by the mellow afterglow of dusk. He could smell late-blooming roses on the air, then spied a rosebush at the corner of the house covered with dark pink blossoms.

When Melissa answered the door, Charles's heart skipped a beat, then resumed at a faster, harder pace. She seemed to have dressed to match the rosebush! She was wearing a filmy, long-sleeved blouse of a color designers would probably call magenta, but which Charles called dark pink. Either way, it played up her blond beauty to perfection.

She wore slim black slacks that clearly revealed the fact that she'd lost all her pregnancy weight. He'd found her sexy even while she was pregnant, but the way she looked now was just like the girl he'd first fallen head-over-heels for back in high school. He could almost picture her in her cheerleading uniform.

Charles wasn't the only one staring, either. Both of them were so busy checking each other out, it was a couple of minutes before they exchanged a single word.

Finally Melissa said, ''Hello, Charles.''

''Hello. You look…terrific.''

Her lashes fluttered down. "Thank you. Please come in."

Charles walked in and got an instant impression of the house as being light and airy, full of greenery and flowers, gleaming wood floors and unfussy white walls. The entryway opened to a small living room and dining room, with a large great room with a fireplace visible at the rear of the house.

With his hands on his hips, he looked around, murmuring, "Nice, Melissa. Very nice. I gather things worked out well with your Schuler's alliance."

Melissa winced a little. "I suppose you read about that in the papers?"

"Sure. And saw a spot on the Channel Five news one night, too." He smiled ruefully. "A follow-up to the big interview, I guess."

Melissa nodded and crossed her arms over her chest in a nervous gesture, almost as if she was cold and trying not to shiver. "Oh, Charles, if you only knew how much I wanted to tell you about that in person. To share my excitement! To thank you for encouraging me to go on with the interview even after Brad showed up and gave us both a nasty shock. I was going to call you from the hospital, but I figured you'd be working on your paper, so I decided to wait till Saturday." She shook her head and looked chagrined. "But we both know what happened that Saturday. We definitely didn't get any talking done."

"No, but that's what we're going to do tonight, right? And, by the way, I don't think I *do* know what happened that Saturday, which is one of the things we're going to talk about," Charles reminded her.

She took a deep breath and expelled it slowly.

"Right. But first why don't you come into the family room and I'll give you a glass of wine?"

"Trying to liquor me up so I'll be more receptive, eh?" he teased, surprised that he was actually starting to feel comfortable enough to joke around. Or was he joking around because he was so nervous?

Melissa laughed, uncrossed her arms and looked marginally more at ease herself. "If it will help, why not? But I won't join you because I'm nursing."

She turned and walked down the hall toward the family room. Charles followed, his gaze taking in the way her hair swayed against her shoulders as she moved—not to mention the way her sexy hips swayed, too. He remembered appreciating the same view that day she was wearing his robe, and his tingling awareness that underneath it was nothing but beautiful bare skin, still pink from her bath.

Suddenly Charles's collar felt too tight and the night too warm. The top button on his polo shirt was already undone. He undid the last two.

"Can I help?" he asked as she walked into the adjoining kitchen, partitioned off from the great room by a large breakfast bar with big, comfortable stools. His voice had come out as an embarrassing croak. He cleared his throat and hoped she hadn't noticed…much.

She turned and looked at him. "Sounds like you really need that drink. My throat gets dry from allergies this time of year, too."

"Yes, there's a lot of stuff floating around in the air," he agreed with her without actually lying. He'd never suffered from allergies a day of his life, but he'd rather she thought he had allergies than randy thoughts about her.

"The baby's asleep, I gather?" he asked, as he watched her pour him a glass of white wine.

"Yes. He generally wakes up again about two."

As soon as she named the wee hour of two in the morning, Melissa looked as though she'd like to take it back. Maybe she thought he'd think she was hinting that he could stay that long....

He said nothing, but quickly stood up and began walking around the room, looking at the pictures and decor, just as anyone might do on their first visit to a friend's new house. But his mind was going a mile a minute. Not to mention his heartbeat. They had till two in the morning to talk...or whatever.

Get a grip, Avery, Charles told himself. *Just because you're so attracted to her you could explode at any moment, doesn't mean the feeling is mutual. Not to mention, she still has some explanations to make.*

When Charles turned around, Melissa was standing just in front of him, holding out the glass of wine. He took it from her, then followed her to the leather sofa. He sat on one end of it, and she sat way down on the other end. She pulled one leg up under her and stretched her arm across the well-padded back of the sofa, facing him.

He thought she looked tense and apprehensive again. Any progress they'd made to loosening up seemed to have vanished.

He figured he probably looked just as uptight to her, so he took a sip of wine, hoping it would help.

He wished he could just take her into his arms and tell her not to worry. The thing was, he was just as worried as she was. He was worried that he wasn't going to like her explanations.

He took another sip of wine.

He wished they didn't have to talk, but he knew they had to. Still, he wished they could just—

"First things first, Charles," Melissa said, which startled him, because it was almost as though she had read his mind.

"Okay," he agreed, not sure what he was agreeing to.

She sighed. "I'm afraid you're not going to find my reasons for lying about Brad very compelling. But, I assure you, they felt compelling to me at the time."

Ah, so that's where she was starting.

"Go on."

"Charles, I had no idea you'd lost your wife in a car accident. In fact, when I told you that Brad was dead, I thought your wife was in New Orleans, paying her respects at a funeral."

Charles nodded. "I realized that early on. I knew you couldn't be that cruel, Melissa," he assured her.

Melissa dropped her head and traced a circle on the sofa with her fingertips. "It's no excuse for lying. But I just wanted you to know I wasn't cruel intentionally...although it *was* cruel. But I didn't think I'd ever see you again after that week, so I didn't think it mattered if I told a lie to...to save my pride."

Charles was surprised. He set down his wineglass on the coffee table. "Your pride? I don't get it, Melissa."

Melissa blushed. "If I explain, I'm going to end up sounding vain and shallow. But I guess it would be the truth—"

"Hey, wait a minute," Charles said, scooting a few inches closer to her. "Don't start putting yourself down. Just be honest, Melissa. Who knows? Maybe if you give me a chance, I'll understand.''

Melissa nodded. ''If anyone would, I suppose it would be you.'' She chewed on her bottom lip a minute, then continued. ''When I was in high school, I had it pretty good. People thought I was…special.''

She looked up then, checking his reaction.

He shrugged. ''They did. And you were.''

She shook her head. ''I'm not asking for compliments.''

''I know you're not. I'm just trying to be totally honest, too.''

She stared at the sofa again for a minute or two, then resumed. ''I had a lot of fun in high school. I enjoyed being pretty and popular. I had a lot of confidence in myself. I had a lot of plans…''

She broke off. Presently she said, ''I was going to go to college and then I was going to start my own business.'' She looked up then, her eyes glistening. ''I was going to make something of myself, Charles. That's what everyone expected of me in high school, but more importantly, that's what I expected of myself.''

He couldn't resist. He scooted closer and took her hand. It was cold, so he started warming it between his own two hands.

''So when I saw you thirteen years later, I was embarrassed by how little I'd lived up to the expectations people had about me. The expectations I had for myself. I'd wasted more than a decade supporting someone else's—''

She stopped, seeming to be looking for the right word.

''Someone else's dreams?'' Charles suggested.

"No, Brad didn't have dreams," Melissa stated flatly. "Let's just say I supported him in his activities. He went to college, but he never took it seriously. He just wanted to play ball. He didn't finish. Then, without an adequate education, he could never get a really good job. He got bored quickly, then quit and sat around the house for months at a time before getting other employment. But he didn't have anything he really cared about deeply, had a passion for...you know? Like your passion for astronomy."

Charles didn't like Brad, to say the least, but he was determined to be fair. "Some people never figure out what they're good at, what they love. I was lucky that I knew what I wanted early on."

"Well, that's very nice of you to say," Melissa said with a faint smile. "But Brad was lazy. He used me and he cheated on me." She looked him earnestly in the eye. "And I *let* him."

Charles took her other hand, hating to see her distressed. "Hey, you don't have to go into all the details if you don't want to." Besides, he knew what a jerk Brad was. Melissa didn't have to tell him.

"I don't want to trash Brad. And I'm not complaining, Charles, or asking you to feel sorry for me," Melissa emphasized.

"I know you're not—"

"I just want you to understand why I lied to you. Quite simply, I was ashamed! I didn't want you to know that I was divorced from the school's most popular guy—who turned out to be not such a great catch, after all—that I was pregnant and broke, living in a cheap apartment, paying off the credit card bills from my husband's affairs, and still working on my college degree. I figured if I told you Brad was dead, that would end any discussions about my private life and I'd be spared the shame of owning up to the fact that I was stupid enough to stay with a man who used me. That I blindly believed in him, supported him and loved him much longer than I should have.''

Charles couldn't help it. He took her face tenderly in his hands and smiled down at her. ''If the most you have to be ashamed of is being too trusting, too supportive and too loving, you're doing *so* much better than most people, Melissa.''

Melissa looked at him, doubtfully, hopefully, as if she wanted to, but couldn't believe what he was saying. ''So, you don't think I was a total idiot? A complete failure?''

Charles stroked her hair, loving the feel of it, the way the light reflected in it. ''When we were in high school, I thought *Brad* was an idiot. It was hard understanding what a great girl like Missy Richardson saw in him.'' Charles shrugged and smiled ruefully. ''But, hey, he was a football star and a lot cooler than a nerd like me who enjoyed math and science.''

''If only high-school girls could see the potential of so-called nerds like you, Charles,'' Melissa said with a sigh. ''They'd be snatched up faster than hundred-dollar bills on the sidewalk.''

He chuckled. ''If only,'' he agreed, as he continued to stroke her hair. Her eyes were drifting shut and he was considering kissing her, when her eyes abruptly opened.

''That Saturday when you came over—''

Charles was way past worrying about Saturday, but he knew Melissa needed to explain and he needed to listen…despite what his body thought it needed!

"I didn't think Brad could get my address that quickly, but he did, and I was so angry when he showed up! He tried to charm me, but I wasn't buying his act anymore. I knew he just wanted to cash in on my recent good luck, but then he put a guilt trip on me by pretending to have fatherly feelings for Avery. He said he'd leave as soon as I let him see the baby, then he followed me into the house without my permission. He even took the baby out of my arms when I expressly told him he wasn't allowed to hold him! Charles, I was so angry, I was ready to cry!"

Charles could see the angry tears in her eyes just from reliving the experience. Now he suspected—no he *knew*—Brad had choreographed the whole thing.

"Did Brad know I was coming over?"

"Yes. He overheard me talking to you on the phone the night before. That's how he got my address, too."

Charles nodded thoughtfully. "Then he left the door open purposely, so I'd walk in on the two of you with Avery and come to the wrong conclusions. And I bought into the act because I *did* think you and Brad were reconciling. I saw the tears in your eyes, but I thought they were sentimental tears. Tears of tenderness."

"Oh, no! Far from it," she said vehemently.

Charles took her face in his hands again and looked deeply into her eyes. "If you knew I got the wrong impression, why didn't you call me and tell me what was really going on between you and Brad?"

Melissa drew his hands away and clasped them tightly in her lap. Now she could direct her gaze elsewhere, which seemed to make it easier for her to talk. "I'd...I'd already lied to you once, and it was a whopper. It was also about Brad. I wasn't sure you'd believe me, or that you cared enough to put up with all my baggage. Besides, I had to get a restraining order to keep Brad away from me and Avery. He finally gave up and moved back to California, but it was kind of ugly for a while. I...I didn't want you involved in all that."

"Well, it was nice of you to try to spare me a little hassle, Missy," Charles told her, allowing a tiny bit of exasperation to slip into his voice. "But you realize that in the meantime, for seven *long* weeks I was imagining you and Brad together. I think I would have preferred the hassles!"

Her head reared up, her eyes moist with emotion. "You could have called *me*, Charles!"

"I wanted to call, but from the way things looked that day... And after what happened—"

"I know," she quickly agreed. Then more quietly, "I *know*."

There was a long pause as they both stared at their clasped hands. Charles wondered if she was as relieved as he was that they'd finally hashed it all out. But...now what?

Presently Melissa looked up shyly. "It's a miracle we ran into each other at the fair."

Charles smiled back. "Yeah, a miracle named Lily. She read an article in the paper about the fair. She knew you'd be there."

"We should give Christopher credit, too," Melissa suggested with a warm twinkle in her eye. "If he hadn't demanded to know what I'd named my baby, which made me finally confess that I'd named him

Avery, I think you would have walked away from me at the fair today and not looked back.''

She was right, but Charles didn't want to think about what might have happened. He was too happy with the way things—by the grace of God and a meddlesome sister and an inquisitive four-year-old son—had actually turned out.

''Why *did* you name him Avery?''

She blushed. ''Well, I couldn't very well name him Charles, now could I? That would have been *way* too obvious.''

Now that all the hard questions had been asked and answered, Charles couldn't resist having a little fun. ''*What* would be obvious, Melissa?''

Her cheeks bloomed a deeper shade of rose, almost matching her blouse. He loved that about her...the way she so easily blushed. ''How crazy I am about you,'' she finally said in a small voice.

Charles's heart sang with joy. He wanted to kiss Melissa more than anything in the world...but first he had a confession of his own.

''Then I guess we're even. 'Cause I'm just as crazy about you.''

Melissa was sure she'd died and gone to heaven. She'd told Charles the truth about herself, and he'd accepted her. He'd seen the good and forgiven the not-so-good. And, best of all, he loved her! Well...at least, that's the way *she* construed the meaning of ''crazy about you.'' She'd better check and make sure.

''Charles? Are you saying...you love me?''

Charles smiled. She loved the way his eyes warmed and his whole face grew tender when he smiled at her.

"That's exactly what I'm saying."

She smiled back. "Then you're right. We're definitely even."

For a long moment, they continued to stare at each other, to smile, to share the wonder of the moment. Then Charles drew her into his arms and just held her there, close to his heart. With her arms wrapped around his neck, Melissa's own heart was beating wildly. She felt precious and beloved. As though she'd come home again after being lost for a long, long time. In Charles's arms, she was finally where she'd always belonged.

She could have stayed that way forever...but she wanted him to kiss her so badly it hurt!

When Charles pulled away far enough to look at her, Melissa saw the same ache of desire reflected in his smoky-green eyes, the same urgency to express their love for each other. Without having to speak, Melissa knew Charles was asking a question. She answered him with an infinitesimal nod of her head and a shy smile.

An ardent expression—the kind every woman on earth longs to see on a man's face at least once in her lifetime—glowed from Charles's eyes and lit up every handsome feature.

He lifted his hand to rest it lightly against her cheek and she couldn't resist leaning into the contact, rubbing her skin against his warm palm. Her eyes drifted shut with the pure pleasure of it, the mutual caress so simple, yet so sensual.

With her eyes closed, she finally felt his lips touch hers. The thrill of that first tentative kiss between lovers, so long awaited and dreamed about, did not disappoint. A frisson of electric awareness thrummed through Melissa's body, sang along every nerve, exploded in every cell.

Charles must have felt the same immediate physical and emotional response. He held her tighter and deepened the kiss, probing the warmth of her mouth with his tongue. His hands began to roam her back, the curve of her waist, the rounded jut of her hips. She loved his touch, his warm, seeking hands.

Melissa's own hands began to wander, to explore. She caressed his smooth, muscled back, his wide shoulders and the strong column of his neck. Then, no longer able to resist, she tugged his shirt out of his jeans and slipped her hands underneath. He shuddered as her hands slid up his taut stomach to his silky chest hair and hard nipples.

"Oh, Melissa. Oh, if you only knew how long I've wanted you to touch me like this."

She trailed kisses along his jawline to his ear, then down his neck. "Since I showed up on your doorstep eight-and-a-half months pregnant?" she teased in a whisper.

He chuckled breathlessly. "Oh, I found you plenty sexy at eight-and-a-half months pregnant, so don't plan on a rest from romance when you're pregnant with *my* baby, Melissa."

Her stomach flip-flopped at this reference to a sure future together, and she reveled joyfully in the fact that she'd finally found a man who *wanted* to get her pregnant!

"Who says I'll want a rest?" she whispered in his ear.

He groaned, pulling her closer. "I had a huge crush on you in high school, you know. The way you looked in that cute little cheerleader uniform made me crazy. You have no idea how many nights I imagined kissing you, holding you.''

Melissa lightly nibbled his ear, then dipped her head to kiss the hollow of his throat and the V of chest exposed by his open collar. ''Sounds to me like we have a lot of time to make up for, then.'' She stood up, took his hand, and drew him to his feet. Smiling, she said, ''I don't believe you've seen the rest of the house.''

Chapter Thirteen

Melissa held on to the two middle fingers of Charles's right hand, guiding him down the hallway to her bedroom. Charles thought he had to be dreaming. When he'd woken up that morning, he never would have imagined that the day would end like this.

When they entered the bedroom, Melissa flipped the light switch and two lamps on either side of her bed gave the room a bright glow. She had a dimmer switch, though, and soon the lighting was softer and more romantic.

Charles grabbed Melissa by the waist and smiled down at her. "I wouldn't have minded the bright light," he told her with a teasing grin. "Like the big bad wolf said to Little Red Riding Hood, 'All the better to see you with, my dear.'"

Melissa laughed self-consciously. "You have to remember, Charles, I just had a baby two months ago."

"I remember. I was there. And it doesn't look like it's hurt your figure one bit, Missy Richardson. In fact, I'll bet you can still get into your cheerleader uniform." He slanted his head to the side and peered down at her consideringly. "You don't still have it, do you?"

She laughed again and swatted his shoulder. "Oh no you don't, Charles Avery. I'm not putting that on for you!"

He laughed, too, surprised by her answer. He had only been teasing and had never expected in a million years that she still had her cheerleading uniform stashed away somewhere. "Don't worry, I was just kidding," he assured her. He looked down at her filmy blouse, at the way her full breasts put a slight strain on the front buttons. "I think you look gorgeous in this rose-colored blouse."

"Thank you, Charles. You always manage to make me feel beautiful. Even when I had swollen ankles and puffy fingers and a basketball-shaped belly," she whispered, then gazed up at him, her lips parted invitingly.

"That's because you *are* beautiful." He bent his head and kissed her. The teasing banter of just moments before quickly escalated into the serious urgency of passion. Charles had never—not even with Annette, whom he'd loved with his whole heart—felt such an overwhelming urge to possess someone, body and soul.

The eager way she returned his kisses, the almost impatient pressure of her soft, pliant body against his, made Charles's blood pulse through his veins like high-octane fuel through the revving engine of a race car. But he didn't want their first coupling, their first physical expression of love, to be a race to the finish line! He wanted it to last a long time, and he particularly wanted to give Melissa as much pleasure as possible.

But she wasn't making it easy for him to slow down.

Her hands were tugging on his shirt, lifting it over his head. Then her fingers tangled in his chest hair, her expression ardent as her gaze roamed over him in a loving and erotic examination.

"Oh, Charles, you're so beautiful."

The chuckle that came out of Charles was strained, his voice broken with passion, his throat constricted with emotion. "Melissa, you're killing me. You make me want to take you right now, and I'm not a wham-bam kind of guy."

"Charles, I *want* you to take me right now... The night's still young. We don't have to stop after the first time, do we?"

Charles was not made of stone. This was an offer he couldn't refuse.

He crushed her against his bare chest and kissed her deeply, passionately, the crisp material of her blouse chafing pleasurably against him. When he slipped his hands under her blouse and took both full breasts in hand at once, she gasped. Then, when he gently teased her nipples with his thumbs, she moaned and arched her back.

With shaky fingers, Charles started to unbutton Melissa's blouse. When he had a little trouble with the tiny, slippery globe-shaped buttons, Melissa helped him, as all the while they stared into each other's eyes and caught their breath in quick, shallow gulps of air.

Soon her blouse was on the floor, followed by her bra. Charles stared down at her full breasts with their rosy-pink nipples and lost his last resolve to go slow. She gave a yelp of pleased surprise when he picked her up and carried her to the bed. Stretched out on the soft, quilted bedspread beside her, he pulled her into his arms and ran his hands over her body in a reverent exploration that quickly blossomed into full-blown passion.

She scooted out of her pants and finally lay naked before him, every inch of her soft, curvy body in full view…and ready for him.

"Now it's your turn," she whispered hoarsely. "Let me see you, Charles."

Charles was as ready as she was…as she'd soon observe. Feeling a little self-conscious, he got off the bed, removed his belt, and began to unbutton the front placket of his jeans. She smiled seductively from the bed.

He grinned. "I feel a little like a stripper."

"You could pass for one. You've got the body," she assured him.

Charles certainly hoped she continued to think so as the jeans dropped to the floor, followed by his jockey shorts.

Melissa had only seen one other naked male body in her life, Brad's. And he had been an athlete. Charles's body was better. He was lean and toned and as sleek as a panther. And as for his arousal…

She patted the spot beside her. "Come back to bed, Charles," she managed to say, while trying to control her breathing.

He hesitated, chewed on the inside of his lip. "I want to get you pregnant, Melissa, but it might be too soon after Avery. Besides, I don't want you walking down the aisle in a maternity gown."

Melissa was speechless and motionless for a moment. She'd been too caught up in the moment to even think about birth control, and even though it sounded as if she'd just received a precursor to a marriage proposal, she already *felt* married to Charles.

"Don't worry," he assured her, reading her thoughts. "I plan to ask you in a much more romantic way...er...later." He grinned. "In the meantime, do you have a condom?"

"Well, I haven't needed a condom for a long, long time," Melissa admitted with a shy smile and blush. "But there might be one with some of the toiletries I threw in a box when I moved from the apartment. I haven't had time to unpack everything yet. Cross your fingers I find one, or you might have to make a run to the drugstore."

Melissa got up, found the box on a bottom shelf in the bathroom, searched through it and discovered a whole package of condoms. She debated about whether or not to take just one condom back to the bedroom or return with the entire package. Feeling brave and slightly naughty, she decided to take the package.

Charles was waiting in the bed when she came back.

"I'm glad you found more than one," he confessed, and Melissa was glad she'd been brave. Charles took her in his arms again and kissed her from head to toe. He teased and nibbled, sucked and gently tugged on her breasts till she thought she'd die from the pleasure of it. She was weak from his kisses and dizzy from the havoc his hands played with her senses. But she tried to give back as good as she got. Judging by Charles's state of arousal, his breathing, his pounding heart, she was succeeding at making him as delirious as he was making her.

Finally he braced himself above her, but instead of entering her, he stroked her moist warmth with his fingers. She arched and moaned and clutched his arms. "Oh, Charles, please," she moaned. "Make love to me. *Now*."

He eased himself inside her and pleasure washed over Melissa like a rolling wave of warm water. She was immersed in sensations so intense and thrilling, she thought she might pass out. But, thank goodness, she didn't; the next few minutes were too good to miss.

She lifted her hips and Charles began to move. He set the rhythm slow and deliberate at first, gazing at her through half-closed eyes, compelling her to look deeply into his soul…as she knew he was looking deeply into hers.

"I love you, Melissa," he whispered.

"I love you, too, Charles."

They held their gazes unwaveringly for a moment, each committing to the other. But then the aching demands of their bodies took over and Charles thrust deeper and faster. Melissa rose to meet each thrust, drawing closer and closer to the wonderful madness of release.

She climaxed and Charles held her as her body rocked and shuddered. Then she felt him climax, too, watching the beautiful intensity of his facial expressions with loving awe.

Afterward, they rested with his arm around her shoulders, his fingers lazily stroking her bare arm, her hand resting, splayed, on his chest.

"Charles?"

He kissed her on the top of her head. "Hmm?"

"Do you know what I wished for that night we saw the first star? The night Avery was born?"

"No, love. What did you wish for?"

She sat up just far enough to turn and look him in the eye. "I wished for *this*, Charles. You and me."

He smiled back. "So did I...in a way. I wished that Avery was mine."

Her eyes filled with tears. "And he will be. As soon as we're married and the adoption papers can be filed."

"Looks like Christopher's going to get his wish, too. A nanny *and* a mommy."

"Mrs. Butters won't mind?" Melissa asked a little anxiously. "We'll definitely still need her since I'll be working. Mostly at home, but there'll be times—"

"Don't worry," Charles assured her. "Mrs. Butters wanted me to wear a tie and bring you candy and flowers. I'm pretty sure she was hoping we'd end up like this." He chuckled. "Well, maybe her imagination didn't go *quite* that far, but I know she wanted us to get together. Lily and Josh feel the same way."

"My parents, too," Melissa revealed. "They're going to be thrilled!" She suddenly thought of something and slapped her hand over her mouth. "Oh *no!*"

Charles looked perplexed, but not alarmed. He could probably see how her eyes were dancing.

"Tell me," he ordered, grabbing her by the shoulders and kissing her neck. "Or I'm make you," he concluded in a throaty growl.

"I'll never tell if you keep that up," Melissa warned him, pulling reluctantly away. "But this is something we maybe should discuss."

He tried to look interested in a discussion, but Melissa could tell that he was ready again for something else. So was she, so she decided she'd better hurry.

"It's Avery's name, Charles. You realize, don't you, that when you adopt him, he'll officially be Avery *Avery?*"

Charles looked stunned for a moment, then laughed out loud. "The poor kid! Have you given him a middle name, Melissa? If you haven't, maybe we should decide on one together. Then, if he finds it too difficult to function with a redundant name like Avery Avery, he can go by his middle name."

She felt herself blushing. "Well, I *did* give him a middle name. But it's...well...it's Charles. His birth certificate reads Avery Charles Richardson."

Charles looked surprised at first, then his expression softened to one of tenderness. "Wow, and for seven weeks I had no idea that you cared about me that much."

"Don't remind me of those awful seven weeks, Charles," Melissa begged him. "I know now I should have called you...but maybe I can make it up to you."

"You don't have to make anything up to me. You weren't happy, either," he said.

Melissa smiled shyly. "You might not want to be that generous, Charles," she suggested in a coy voice. "You see...I was thinking of making it up to you by modeling my cheerleading uniform."

By the look on Charles's face, Melissa knew she'd made a suggestion that surprised him...but also most definitely delighted him. "My teenage dream come true," he murmured dryly, then crossed his arms behind his neck and lounged against the headboard.

With his green eyes glittering and his mouth curved in an amused but expectant smile, he proclaimed, ''Let the games begin!''

One year later

CHARLES ROLLED the barbecue grill into a corner of the patio and took off his World's Greatest Dad apron. He walked to the edge of the patio and looked out over the lawn. Standing with his hands lightly resting on his hips, he watched his family playing soccer.

Christopher was a tall five-year-old with more team sports ability than Charles had ever had as a child, so he had to take it easy when he kicked the ball to Sarah and Daniel. Avery, a sturdy toddler, was happy just to run in the same general direction as his oldest brother, even though he wasn't on the same team. Mrs. Butters and Melissa rounded out the competition and served as referees and Band-Aid dispensers when someone got a scratch.

They had been playing since dinner while Charles had been cleaning up the mess from the barbecue. It was his opinion that since he did the cooking, he ought to do the cleaning up, too. Although he occasionally offered, he seldom was allowed to do dishes in the house. A barbecue was—again in his opinion—ladies' night off.

By dusk on this wonderful, mild evening after a warm September day, the kids had finally got tired enough to collapse on the two blankets Melissa had spread on the grass. The sun was setting over the Great Salt Lake and a golden glow was spreading over the foothills like a smear of orange marmalade on a bagel. Daniel was sitting in between Melissa's legs, her chin resting on his rusty colored hair. Avery and Christopher were examining a caterpillar on a leaf Christopher had plucked from a nearby lilac bush. Sarah was sitting in Mrs. Butters's lap on the other blanket, her face snuggled into Mrs. Butters's ample bosom, ready to fall asleep.

Melissa turned, saw Charles standing at the top of the lawn and beckoned him over. Charles didn't need persuading. He'd just been savoring the moment, thinking about how lucky he was, before actually joining the people who were the reason he thought of himself as the luckiest guy on the face of the earth.

As he approached the group, Avery looked up and immediately lost interest in the caterpillar. "Daddy!" he shouted with remarkable clarity, considering he was only fourteen months old. He ran toward Charles, lifting his arms to be picked up.

Charles met him halfway, picked him up and threw him over his head. Avery gurgled and laughed while airborne, causing a drop of saliva to fall right on Charles's nose.

Christopher saw the wet welcome Charles had received from Avery and laughed out loud. "Dad, he hit you with a loogie!"

"Christopher, such language," Mrs. Butters remonstrated, but couldn't help laughing herself. As she chortled, Mrs. Butters's bosom jiggled and stirred the drowsy Sarah, who looked up sleepily and smiled at Charles. Her smile and her deep-brown eyes always reminded him of Annette.

Annette. Charles would always remember his first wife fondly. Always regret that she couldn't watch the children she loved so much grow up. But even though Christopher was the only one of the children who had a real, although fading, memory of his mother, Melissa honored Annette's memory by talking about her with the children whenever it seemed appropriate and keeping her picture out so they wouldn't forget what she looked like. But to all the children, Melissa was now "Mommy."

Besides, Charles had a feeling Annette *did* look in on them from time to time…and liked what she saw.

"We're watching for the first star, Dad," Sarah told him. "I'm gonna make a wish. Mommy says wishing on the first star of the night works better than wishbones or wishing wells or anything."

"But remember Sarah, the wishes don't always come true overnight," Melissa reminded her, obviously not wanting Sarah to be disappointed if she wished for a pony and didn't find one in the backyard the next morning. "You have to be patient." She looked at Charles and smiled. "And sometimes you have to work really hard for your most special wishes to come true."

Christopher plopped down next to Mrs. Butters, and Charles lowered himself and Avery to a spot next to Melissa and Daniel.

"I got a call from Grant Schuler today," Melissa told him.

Charles spread his legs out in front of him, crossing his ankles, and Avery climbed over them, back and forth, back and forth, like a restless little mini-mountaineer.

Charles looked at Melissa expectantly. "You never mentioned anything at dinner."

She laughed. "Dinner was a little chaotic, if you

recall. I thought I'd wait till the kids had calmed down a little.''

''What did he say?''

She looked at the sunset, at the pink rays shooting up through clouds that streaked across the sky. Her face was awash in color, making her look as if she was blushing. For Charles, the sight of a blushing Melissa was familiar and endearing.

''He said he thought it would work fine if I cut back my hours to twenty a week. Everything's in place for next year's new products and sales are great.'' She turned to face Charles. ''He knows I love Missy's Kid Cuisine and the work that goes with it, but he knows I want to spend more time with my family, too.''

''And he knows that if he didn't agree with everything you said, you could take Missy's Kid Cuisine to some other large baby-food company. You still own the name and the original recipes, which are still the most popular. I'm sure you could work as much or as little as you wanted, Melissa, as long as you got the job done. And Grant knows you'll get the job done.''

Melissa nodded. ''Yep, that pretty much sums it up. But I wanted to make sure he understood that there'd be times I'd simply turn off my phone and become available only to my family.'' The smile she gave him was intimate as her voice lowered. ''Especially since I plan to increase our family in the near future.''

Charles smiled and said nothing. He knew Melissa thought getting rid of some of the stress of developing into such a pivotal person at Schuler's would help her conceive. He just hoped it was true. They'd been trying to have another baby for six months. She said they had "his and hers" kids and now they ought to have "theirs," just like that Lucille Ball movie from the sixties where two families combined, then they created their own little additions.

Charles didn't think of the children as his and hers, and he knew Melissa didn't either, really. But he did know she wanted to have *his* child to make their family complete.

Charles wanted to have a child with Melissa, too, very much, but he really considered Avery his. He'd been there when he was born. He'd raised him as his own since he was two months old. In fact, it sometimes took Charles by surprise if someone referred to Avery as Brad's biological child...although that seldom happened, and usually only when someone from Melissa's family said, "Gee, he doesn't look anything like Brad. He looks like Missy." Charles simply forgot that Avery wasn't his biological offspring. He was his son in every other way and that was all that mattered.

"Look, there's the first star!" shouted Christopher, standing and hitching up his loose shorts at the same time. "Everybody close your eyes and make a wish!"

Charles closed his eyes and made his usual wish. It didn't take long, but when he opened his eyes, Melissa's eyes were already open and gazing at him with a mischievous gleam lurking in those baby blues.

"What did you wish for?" she asked him.

"What I always wish for," he answered immediately. "The same thing *you* always wish for." He leaned over and whispered in her ear. "A baby...right?"

Melissa shrugged her shoulders and looked unconcerned. "Nope. Not this time."

Charles's brow furrowed. "Honey, I hope you're not giving up. It's only been six months, you know, and—"

"Oh, I'm not giving up," she informed him breezily.

"You've just decided that wishing on stars doesn't work?" he asked her, again speaking low enough so as not to be heard by the children.

"No, it's not that," she said. "It works all right. Or, at least, *something's* making my most cherished wishes come true."

Charles stared at her, perplexed.

She appeared to relish his look of confusion and laughed heartily and so infectiously, Charles couldn't help a wide smile. Melissa's laugh drew the attention of all the kids and Mrs. Butters, too. They watched and wondered what was going on.

"Charles, my dear husband, you're a *brain*. You're a scientist. You've invented state-of-the-art lenses that have made the exploration of the heavens as easy as pie for anyone who can afford to buy a backyard telescope. But you still don't know what I'm talking about?"

It suddenly dawned on Charles what she meant about something making all her most cherished wishes come true. Could it be...? Was it possible she was—?

Before Charles could get the words out, Christopher sidled up next to him and said in his most serious voice, "Gee, Dad, I think Mom's trying to tell you that I'm gonna have another little brother or sister.''

Charles wasn't sure how he knew, but Christopher definitely knew that's exactly what they'd been hoping for. Charles turned to Melissa for corroboration, saw it in the happy glow that spread over her face and in the soft glistening of emotion in her eyes.

''Christopher's right, Charles,'' Melissa admitted. She looked around at everyone and smiled through her tears. ''I'm going to have a baby.''

Mrs. Butters got teary and the children cheered. Avery looked as though he didn't know why he was cheering, but it was fun, so he figured what the heck. Charles simply took his wife in his arms and kissed her.

''Wishes do come true, Charles,'' she whispered in his ear. ''But it was *you* who made the magic happen. You have given me everything I've ever wanted.''

''You think I'm a brain, Melissa,'' Charles whispered back. ''You think I'm smart because I invented a special telescope lens. But the smartest thing I ever did was hire a temporary nanny.''

Melissa nodded her agreement, too happy for words.

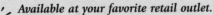
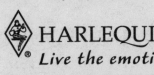

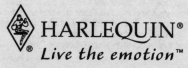

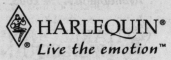

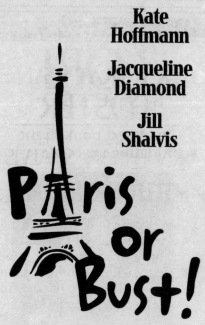

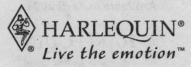